Accidental CEO

Bart Paden

TABLE OF CONTENTS

A Note to the Reader

Hi there. Before we dive in, I want to let you in on something: this isn't your typical leadership manual.

In fact, calling me a "leader" back when I started would have been a stretch, and that's exactly why I'm writing this. I stumbled, fumbled, and basically tripped my way into becoming a CEO. Consider this book a personal, honest journey rather than a polished handbook. I'll share the good decisions, the bad ones, and the downright ridiculous ones.

Why? Because I wish someone had told me these stories when I was a few steps behind where I am now.

If you're looking for bullet-point perfection, you might be in the wrong place. But if you don't mind a little self-deprecating humor and some painfully honest moments, I think you'll find something valuable here. Whether you're running a company, leading a team, or just trying to figure out what's next, this book is about the messy, meaningful process of becoming someone worth following.

Let's start at the beginning... or, at least, my beginning.

.

Chapter 1

The Accidental Part

I didn't plan on becoming a CEO.

That might sound strange coming from someone writing a leadership book, but the truth is, this entire journey started with a little curiosity, a lot of uncertainty, and just enough desperation to say yes to things I had no idea how to do.

It all started in the late 1990s when I discovered the internet. Not in a tech-guru, "I'm going to change the world" kind of way. More like, "Wait, people can make websites from home and get paid for it?" I was a broke college kid and figured I could probably learn enough HTML to fake it until I made it. So that's exactly what I did.

The first time I got paid to build a website, I thought, "This is it. I'm rich." It was something like $200, but in 1998, that was gold to me. More importantly, it gave me a taste of something I hadn't felt in a long time, confidence.

Now, I wasn't someone who struggled in school. Actually, I was a straight-A student and graduated near the top of my class in 1992. I was pretty smart, math and science made sense to me. I loved art and design, and I could write a solid research paper when I needed to. Looking back, I think I had leadership instincts even then, I just didn't know that's what they were. I thought I was just bossy or organized. Turns out, it was something deeper that would surface again later in life.

After college, I landed a job with Precious Moments in Carthage, Missouri. Not because I had a stacked résumé or a fancy degree, I didn't, but because two special people, Terri and Ted, saw something in me. They took a chance, and that chance changed everything.

As part of the interview process, I was asked to write a press release for an upcoming event. I didn't even know what a press release was. I stared at the assignment for a while, then decided to do something else entirely. I built a small website, three or four pages, announcing the event. It included event details, a few images, and contact information. No bells and whistles. Just a clean, clear presentation of what people needed to know. It wasn't what they asked for, but it showed what I could do. That bold little detour got me hired.

I started in the Marketing Department and spent the next four and a half years figuring things out in real time. We didn't have a huge digital strategy back then, honestly, almost no one did, but I had enough curiosity and drive to learn what we needed as we went. By the time I left, I had helped grow their online sales from $20,000 a year to over $1.2 million. It wasn't about genius. It was about curiosity, effort, and actually caring about the outcome.

But things took a turn. Eventually, I was reassigned to the IT department. Suddenly, I was troubleshooting hardware, crawling under desks to run wires, and freezing in a server room that felt like a meat locker. It wasn't what I signed up for, and it wasn't where I was supposed to be.

That's when I knew it was time to go.

I didn't quit in a blaze of glory. I negotiated a termination. Since the new responsibilities weren't part of my original job description, I qualified for unemployment benefits. That money, modest as it was, became the lifeline that gave my family just enough room to breathe while I figured out what was next.

I tell people it felt like I jumped out of an airplane holding either a parachute or a lunchbox, I wasn't sure which. But I jumped anyway.

There was no business plan. No investors. No backup strategy. Just a beat-up laptop, a few freelance clients, and a deep determination not to go backward.

Slowly, it grew.

At first, I was just trying to survive. But over time, I realized something bigger was happening. This wasn't just about websites and logos. It was about building trust. Helping people solve problems. Showing up. And eventually... leading.

I didn't set out to be a leader, but leadership found me.

And I remember the exact moment it started to take shape.

There was a young guy I knew, just about to get married. He was raw, still learning, but incredibly talented. Honestly, he was already a better designer than I was. I saw something in him and made a decision: I brought him on. Not because the business was booming, but because I believed in building something that could grow beyond just me. I even gave up part of my own income so he could have health insurance. That was my first real and significant leadership decision, the sacrificial kind. The kind where you put someone else's needs ahead of your own. That moment shifted how I viewed leadership. It wasn't about power or position, it was about responsibility.

I still made mistakes, of course. I undercharged. I overpromised. I said yes to projects that made no sense just to keep the lights on. I was figuring it out one client at a time, learning how to build a business while also learning how to lead.

But that early decision, to invest in someone else at personal cost, became a kind of blueprint. It showed me what kind of leader I wanted to be. Not the boss barking orders from a corner office, but someone willing to go first. Willing to sacrifice. Willing to bet on people, even before they fully believed in themselves.

And somewhere in that chaos, I started to understand what leadership really is.

It's not about being the smartest person in the room. It's about being the most grounded. It's not about telling people what to do. It's about listening, lifting, and walking alongside them. It's about seeing people, not just their output. It's about building something that lasts, not just for your own success, but for the success of others.

This book isn't here to show off the polished version of that journey. It's here to walk you through the raw parts, the funny parts, the broken parts, and the breakthroughs. Because I think leadership is less about the mountaintop moments and more about what happens in the climb.

So if you've ever felt like you're figuring it out as you go, welcome. You're not alone.

This is the story of how I accidentally became a CEO, and how I grew, over time, into someone worth following.

Chapter 2

What He Gave Me

I think I realized sometimes you have to take a risk and bet on yourself.

But for me, that risk didn't come from a place of confidence. It came from a collapse. And sometimes that's where the most honest leadership begins.

The final stretch of my time at Precious Moments was unraveling at the same time my personal life was collapsing. I wasn't just going through a divorce, I was living through betrayal. The person I had committed my life to was having an affair with someone I considered a close friend. Not just any friend, but a leader in our church small group. Someone I trusted. Someone I prayed with. The fallout wasn't just relational, it was spiritual. It felt like my entire foundation had been pulled out from under me.

I stayed at work and tried to hold it together. But behind the scenes, I was in survival mode. I was dealing with lawyers, courtrooms, and a custody battle that felt endless. I didn't know how to make sense of it. I just knew I couldn't stay in that life anymore.

The divorce became final shortly after I negotiated my termination. The job had shifted far away from what I was hired to do, and I worked out a deal that allowed me to leave with unemployment benefits. That small bit of financial stability became the runway I needed, barely, to try something on my own.

So there I was. Unemployed. Alone. A dad fighting for time with his kids. No plan. No savings. No fallback.

All I had was a belief, just enough to move forward, that maybe I could build something from the rubble.

I started taking on small freelance jobs. Web projects. Design work. Anything that paid. I put my name out there and hoped the next gig would come through. The risk was enormous. The weight was heavy. There was no guaranteed outcome, only the desperate kind of faith that shows up when your back is against the wall.

And then something unexpected happened.

In November of 2003, I met Carie.

She came into my life during the most unstable season I'd ever known. I had nothing to offer her. No job title. No house. No real sense of direction. But somehow, she saw something in me. She didn't try to fix me, she simply walked beside me. She believed in a future I couldn't yet see.

We got married in March of 2004. That same year, I officially started the business.

The custody battle continued, and in September of 2004, tragedy struck when Jennifer, my ex-wife, was killed. The legal battle ended, but the emotional journey didn't. Carie didn't just embrace my boys, she became Mom, without us even asking. She stepped into their world with full-hearted love, grace, and intention.

And our story didn't end there.

Within two years, I adopted Oakley, Carie's daughter, as my own. We didn't just blend families. We became one. One mom. One dad. Three amazing kids. One roof. One new beginning. God didn't just mend a broken path, He erased it, and He laid down new ground beneath our feet. Solid ground. Family-shaped ground. It was redemption in its most complete form.

The business was never about chasing success. It was about survival.

It was born in the fire, refined by the need to lead when life gave me no other choice.

It was about giving my family a future.

It was about building something that reflected the second chance I'd been given.

And that's when I started learning what leadership really meant.

It wasn't about having all the answers. It wasn't about climbing a corporate ladder. It was about making intentional choices when nothing felt secure. It was about showing up, even when I didn't feel qualified. It was about aligning my words with my actions and letting my values, not my fear, lead the way.

That's where servant leadership took root. Not because I read about it, but because I lived it. I didn't want to be the kind of leader who barked from the back, I wanted to be in the trenches. Shoulder to shoulder. Carrying the weight too.

Looking back, I can see it now.

God gave me exactly what I needed, not what I would have asked for, and certainly not what I expected. But what He gave me was better.

He gave me pain that produced clarity.

He gave me people who reminded me I didn't have to do it alone.

He gave me purpose that outweighed the pressure.

He gave me a path.

And all I had to do was walk it, even when I couldn't see more than a few steps ahead.

That's how leadership started for me, not at the summit, but on the shaky path out of ruin.

Chapter 3

The Long Road Alone

Grinding Through the Years

Those years between 2004 and 2010 were defined by one word: grind. My days started at seven in the morning, getting the kids to school, and from there I was immediately on the clock. I would design and code all day, managing projects and communicating with team members scattered across the world until the kids came home. Then I shifted into the roles of husband, father, and coach until bedtime. Once the house quieted, I went right back to work, often until two or three in the morning. Then I'd sleep for a handful of hours, get up, and do it again. Wash, rinse, repeat.

I was exhausted all the time, but I didn't let it stop me. In truth, I didn't know how to stop. Sleep never came easily anyway. It wasn't until 2024 that I was diagnosed with sleep apnea, but looking back, I believe it had been with me all along. That hidden condition explained a lot about why rest never felt restorative and why I believed I could simply power through without consequence. In those days, the ability to work twenty hours straight felt like a strength. Only later would I learn it came with a price tag that would show up in my health years down the road.

The work itself wasn't light. One of my earliest contracts was with Motive Movie Marketing, where I built projects for Disney, Icon Films, and a handful of music labels. I was a tiny fish in a very big pond, building websites for Hollywood studios from a bedroom office in flyover country. The pressure was enormous, but it was also refining. I specifically worked on campaigns for The Chronicles of Narnia from

Disney and The Passion of the Christ for Icon Films. With the latter, our team took a major studio investment that multiplied several times over through targeted group marketing through targeted group marketing. It still amazes me that I got to be part of that effort from my small corner of the world.

The expectations were extreme. Today, design and code are fluid, with flexible layouts and responsive systems. Back then, everything was in line. CSS wasn't even a thing yet. I was handed finished studio designs and expected to translate them perfectly into web pages. And when I say "perfectly," I mean it. Studio art directors would send notes asking me to move a graphic two pixels in one direction or another. Two dots on the screen. That was the level of precision they demanded.

At first, it was maddening. But over time, that discipline became training. I learned to find satisfaction in the tedium, to see those tiny corrections not as insults but as tools sharpening me. That season taught me to respect detail and to build systems that could handle exacting standards. It was the same discipline I would later expect from my team. Those two-pixel adjustments were preparing me for the next twelve to fifteen years, shaping how I would lead people whose skills far exceeded my own.

Carrying the Weight Together

Before the daycare years, our roles were actually flipped. Carie spent years selling cutting tools to machine shops while I was a "designer." She was the one walking shop floors; I was the one pushing pixels. Later, when we leaned fully into being self-employed, she opened a daycare downstairs, and I worked upstairs building the first iteration of what became Midwestern Interactive. It wasn't typical by most people's expectations, but it worked because we were aligned.

Midwestern Interactive (MWI) was the software firm I co-founded in 2012 but had been building since 2005. What started as a solo operator in a home office turned into more than 100 diverse humans in multiple locations, testing everything I believed about leadership and culture.

We were both tapped all the time. Three kids, a home, cars, bills, and the weight of building something new pressed on us constantly. There were days, weeks, and months when I couldn't explain how we made it through. The pressure was relentless, but the provision was just as steady. We never went without. We never lacked what we needed.

The only explanation I have is God's hand. I can't take ownership of any part of the story that carried us through those years. Looking back over the whole thirty-two-year timeline, it's clear: God did it all. It was His path for me and for my family. That conviction didn't make the grind easier, but it made it worth it.

Learning to Be Second

Those years also taught me a truth I've never let go of: I'm not special because I own something or lead something. No one is. The grind of working alone, the exhaustion, the constant dependence on God's provision, all of it birthed the conviction I've lived by ever since: I am second.

I could never look back at those years and pretend I had done it all myself. God was carrying me and my family the whole way. That reality put me in a posture of service. Leadership was never about power, ego, or even financial gain. It was about building something greater than myself, not just a company, but a culture.

To this day, when I see someone achieve a dream, win a championship, or even notch a small victory in life, I celebrate it. Even if they beat me, good for them. That posture, choosing to celebrate others instead of centering myself, became the reason I existed as a leader. And I believe it's also why I found so much success in what some would call a short timeline.

Chapter 4

From the Beginning

When I look back at the early years, I can see a clear dividing line. For a long time, I was just doing the work, building websites from a home office, keeping clients happy, and trying to survive. But the moment I began to gather a team around me, the weight shifted. I wasn't only responsible for outcomes anymore. I was responsible for people.

From the beginning, my goal wasn't to build a company for its own sake. Plenty of people start businesses with growth or profit as the target. That was never enough for me. My goal was to live out servant leadership through the culture we created. Accountability and service weren't strategies I added later, they were in my DNA, and they shaped everything that followed.

I knew a company's culture doesn't appear by accident. It forms in the early decisions, in the way leaders respond to pressure, and in the values that get reinforced when things go wrong. These were the moments when my posture as a servant leader either took root or withered. Looking back now, I can see the fingerprints of those decisions everywhere.

This chapter is about those first defining stories. They weren't glamorous. They didn't make headlines. But they show what was at the core of the company from the very beginning: service, protection, and accountability.

When the tornado hit Joplin in May of 2011, our community was put in a blender. It wasn't just destruction, it was disorientation. People didn't know where to go, what resources existed, or how to connect their needs to the flood of help pouring in.

The call came from a friend, the director of a local nonprofit. Their mission was already to serve the community, and when the tornado hit, their focus shifted overnight. They asked if I could drop everything and build a system to connect needs to resources. I said yes, and my team followed my lead.

For me, that decision wasn't some bold, heroic moment. It was simple: this is what we do when our community needs help. Servant leadership doesn't posture. It turns effort outward.

The pace inside our office during those three days was electric. We felt the weight of the darkness pressing in from outside, but we stayed locked on the goal. High energy, high pressure, no slack. That's normal in software, but here, the stakes were human. If we shipped this system, people might actually get help faster. If we failed, the cracks in the relief effort would swallow real families.

For 72 hours, we ran 24x7. We stretched our pace, our skills, and our endurance further than ever before. The platform launched, and I had to step outside just to catch my breath. We had accomplished the mission. People had a better chance at getting what they needed in the most dire situation any of us had ever known.

I wasn't proud of myself. I was proud of my team. Not one of them had lost a home. Not one of them had a personal stake in the recovery. They gave everything they had because that's what servant leaders do: they give until they're empty. And I did the same. Every last ounce.

On Monday, I led us back into client work. No celebration. No victory lap. That's what we do.

Looking back, I see now what Robert Greenleaf, the original voice behind modern servant leadership, meant by stewardship. A servant leader isn't chasing recognition; they take responsibility for the people and communities around them, even when no one's asking. Larry

Spears, who later articulated Greenleaf's work into a clear leadership framework, described this posture as "community building," one of the core pillars of servant leadership. That's what this was. We didn't just build a website. We built a lifeline.

The cost was real. Three days of exhaustion. A year of follow-up improvements and support while balancing our workload. Potentially strained client timelines. But the payoff was beyond measure: a community that had a fighting chance and a team that learned, firsthand, what it meant to pour out everything in service of others.

Servant leadership shows itself in the small cracks most people overlook. Big institutions stepped in after the tornado, but their help took time. Insurance checks didn't show up overnight, and families were left waiting. In the meantime, real needs went unmet, a window to keep the rain out, a set of tires so someone could get to work.

That gap became the heart of Restore Joplin. A simple logo, a heart with a bandage, gave people a way to rally. We raised $250,000, and every dollar went to those in-between needs. Nothing glamorous. Nothing headline-worthy. Just the kind of ordinary faithfulness that keeps people moving one step forward.

This is the part of servant leadership that rarely gets attention. It isn't about standing out or being called a hero. It's about elevating others quietly, often anonymously, and meeting them right where they are. The power isn't in the size of the gift but in the posture behind it: what can I do, with what I have, to lift someone else?

That same posture played out inside the company, too. Servant leadership wasn't just for disaster response. It was how I chose to lead every day.

Pappa Bart

Ryan was one of our engineers, smart, committed, steady. He was working on a project for a client when things suddenly turned volatile.

The owner, who had been mostly detached, inserted himself into the situation. He brought along his girlfriend, who also served as the office manager. Neither of them had been involved in the work, but they came in swinging. On a call, they made claims that were flat-out fabrications and laced their accusations with thinly veiled threats.

You just don't talk to my people that way.

I stopped the call. Cleared everyone else out until it was just me and the owner. I told him plainly that a line had been crossed, and it would not be crossed again. There wasn't yelling or posturing, but there was no mistaking the seriousness. He heard me. He apologized. And from that moment forward, the project returned to the work it was meant to be.

That moment wasn't about me proving strength. It was about Ryan knowing he was safe, that someone would step in when things turned unjust. Servant leadership isn't only about serving the client, it's about protecting your people when they're in the right. Dignity has to be shielded. Without it, trust collapses.

A transactional leader might have handled that call differently. They might have absorbed the false accusations, turned on their own employee, or sacrificed dignity in order to keep the client happy. It's a short-term play: save the account at the cost of the team. But that's not leadership, that's fear. Servant leadership takes a different posture. It protects the people doing the work. It creates a climate of justice where trust can grow.

That day, Ryan walked away knowing I had his back. He started calling me "Pappa Bart." And I believe that shaped him just as much as it shaped me. Years later, at the end of my time at MWI, he pulled me aside. He said, "I want to continue to carry the torch for you." That said everything. He didn't just want to do good work, he wanted to carry forward the kind of leadership he had experienced.

Accountability – A Two-Way Street

Kevin was a client you couldn't forget. He was six-foot-four, with a cowboy hat and a booming voice that could fill the building. When he came to see us, you knew it. He believed in us, but he expected results, and he didn't shy away from saying so.

One project started to slip, and the mistakes were on Mike, one of our engineers. He was talented but young, and at that point, his ego was outpacing his execution. He had dropped several balls, and this time Kevin noticed.

I wasn't in the building that day, but I didn't need to be. Kevin's voice carried, and the story of that meeting made the rounds quickly. He called out the failure directly, laying it plain with the kind of authority only a man like him could bring. Mike had no excuse, and I didn't give him one. He faced Kevin himself, absorbed the weight of the accountability, and promised to fix it.

At the time, the truth was Mike wasn't open to being led. Pride and ego were getting in his way, and they created a separation between him and the culture I was trying to build. Sometimes servant leadership means protecting, like I did with Ryan. Other times, it means stepping back and letting someone face the weight of their own decisions. Shielding Mike would have spared him in the moment, but it wouldn't have helped him grow.

As soon as I heard what had taken place, I called Kevin myself. I didn't try to downplay it or make excuses. I thanked him for speaking up. We deserved to hear everything he told us. He was right to expect better, and I wanted him to know his voice mattered. That honesty only strengthened the relationship. Kevin didn't lose respect for us because of the mistake, he gained more because we owned it.

Years later, Mike approached me and apologized. It had taken time, but he eventually recognized the arrogance and damage of those years. He did his best to reconcile. That moment didn't erase the cost of his choices, but it did remind me that accountability, paired with truth, can still plant seeds that bear fruit, sometimes much later than we expect.

The culture I was shaping wasn't defined by one big moment. It was formed by dozens of decisions like these. Protecting when it was right. Exposing when it was needed. Stepping into the gaps, whether for a community shattered by disaster or an employee who needed the weight of accountability.

That is the essence of servant leadership. Not theory. Not slogans. Just a steady posture of service, justice, truth, and care, lived out in real moments with real people.

Chapter 5

Building Culture

Values on paper don't make a culture. You can write them down, put them on the wall, or rehearse them in meetings, but until they are lived, they're just words. After the DNA of servant leadership was set, service, protection, and accountability, the next test was whether we could make those values real.

When I say we in this chapter, I mean the team. They were the ones who carried these rhythms and lived them out every day. My role was to set the DNA and lead with conviction, but the culture was theirs as much as it was mine.

This was the season where culture took shape. Not as theory, but as practice. The systems, the ceremonies, the boundaries, and the investments were all ways of telling people they mattered. From the outside, some of it looked ordinary, huddles, celebrations, transparency, but inside, it was the difference between survival and trust. It was what made us strong enough to carry one another when the weight got heavy.

Rhythms & Ceremonies

Culture is built on what you repeat, not what you announce. For our team, the heartbeat of that repetition was communication.

We held daily stand-ups and huddles because the work demanded it. In a business as complex as ours, there were always dozens of moving parts, and just as many opportunities to let something slip. I used to say all the time, "Don't drop the ball." Those meetings were how we made sure of it. They gave everyone clarity on priorities, surfaced issues before they became problems, and kept people from being left on islands. Most companies leave people guessing. We didn't.

Looking back, the systems we had in place looked a lot like SCRUM or other Agile project-management ceremonies. Daily stand-ups, backlog grooming, sprint reviews all of that eventually became part of our formal playbook once we installed a project-management team. But long before we had names for them, we had the instincts. We knew we needed to communicate daily, to make priorities visible, and to create space for constant course correction. Servant leadership demanded it.

But here's the real reason we did it: I knew the human behind the task mattered more than the task itself. The policies, the systems, the procedures, even the celebrations, weren't about efficiency alone. They were about dignity. They were about telling every person on the team, "You matter." Yes, the work had to get done, but the greater work was showing people they weren't just cogs in a process. They were seen, valued, and part of something bigger.

The celebrations layered on top of that backbone. Friday brunch, birthdays, new houses, anniversaries, even Beer:30, all of it mattered, but it was secondary. The celebrations reinforced belonging. The rhythms created trust.

And that consistency is what made the culture solid. People didn't have to wonder if they were seen, if their voice mattered, or if someone else knew what they were carrying. The rhythms made sure no one was left behind, and the ceremonies reminded them they were more than just their work.

MWI Cares

As the team grew, I realized two things were true. First, people don't always like talking with the boss about their problems, especially personal ones. Even though I worked hard to foster openness, there were still barriers. Second, I wasn't equipped to carry everything myself. I wasn't a woman, and as our team grew to include incredible women, I knew they needed safe spaces I couldn't fully provide.

That's where MWI Cares came from. It wasn't just another HR program. It was an intentional structure that created safe, trusted channels for people to get help. In an industry like tech, where studies consistently show women face higher rates of burnout, attrition, and exclusion, it mattered even more to build something that said, "You belong here, and your needs matter."

MWI Cares created space for all of it. Sometimes that meant covering significant medical expenses. Sometimes it meant paying for counseling. Sometimes it was smaller, quieter needs that never made headlines but made all the difference in someone's life. The point wasn't the size of the expense. The point was that no one had to carry their burdens alone.

The clearest picture of this was what came to be known as the crying couch. One of our designers hit a breaking point. The details aren't mine to share, but what mattered was that they weren't left to fall apart in isolation. Work stopped, and presence took priority. I sat with them, listened, and carried what I could. No fixing, no rushing, just being there.

That's what servant leadership looks like. Not rushing past pain, but giving it space. Not treating people like a task to be managed, but like a human to be honored. The crying couch was never part of an employee manual, but it defined us more than any policy ever could.

MWI Cares wasn't about fixing everything. It was about making sure every person knew there was a path to care. It told the team: You are more than the code you write or the designs you ship. You are human, and you matter.

The 80/20 Rule

One of the most important decisions I made as a leader was to build margin into the way we worked. For us, it became the 80/20 rule.

The idea was simple: if 100% of your effort goes into production, you leave no time for progress. People burn out. Growth stalls. Creativity disappears. That wasn't the kind of culture I wanted to build.

The 80/20 rule gave the team permission and accountability to keep moving forward in both work and life. It meant space for learning, refining, and building better systems. It meant they weren't chained to the urgent at the expense of the important. Paradoxically, when we pulled back from chasing productivity at all costs, productivity actually increased dramatically.

It also created space for leadership itself. Some business leaders today have lost sight of this. They believe if you're not producing, you're nothing. But that isn't true. Teams need leaders. Teams also need managers. Those roles may not be billable from a revenue perspective, but they are productive in the truest sense. They foster progress by growing the people around them.

This wasn't a one-time idea. It was daily. I used these rhythms to keep my hand on the pulse of the team. Were they making progress? Were they thriving? Were they carrying weight in a sustainable way? The 80/20 rule gave me the framework to check in and make adjustments before cracks formed.

And the result was unmistakable. When you do more than tell people they matter, when you actually structure their time to prove it, it leaves a mark. People feel safer. They feel freer to be creative. They burn out less. That was the whole point.

Growth, Health, and Wellness

We didn't want to build workers. We wanted to build people. That meant investing in their growth, health, and wellness as much as their output.

When growth required it, we invested. That meant covering certifications, training, and other opportunities that helped people move forward. These weren't blank checks for personal whims, there had to be a foundation of skill already in place, and the growth had to matter. If development was necessary for their advancement and for the health of the team, we funded it. Our aim was simple: keep people advancing, not stagnating.

Health was just as important. A lot of it was woven into the events we already loved. Fitness is hard, but it gets easier when you do it side by side with others. We encouraged ten-minute walks every hour. Most of the time, those walks weren't just about steps on a counter, they became opportunities for conversations, relationships, and problem-solving. Some of the best ideas came while moving.

We even created themes to keep this front and center. Every May, we had "Be Kind to Your Mind" month. During that season, the emphasis shifted to mental health. We built in educational sessions, trainings, and conversations that had little to do with client work but everything to do with growing as whole humans.

The conviction behind it was simple. People matter more than the task. They definitely matter more than profits. Trading a little cash for a healthier, stronger, more whole human is always the right decision. Trading a human's well-being for profit is always wrong.

Transparency

For me, transparency was never about rare moments of revelation. It was about consistency. I didn't wait for a crisis to pull people in. I shared as often as I could, finances, strategy, opportunities, struggles. If a decision was going to affect the team, they deserved to know about it.

What is there really to hide in business? Every choice a leader makes lands on the people doing the work. Pretending otherwise doesn't protect them; it just blindsides them. I wanted the team to know the reality they were living in, good, bad, or uncertain.

That consistency built trust that has lasted far beyond the years we worked together. Many of the relationships I still have with former staff trace back to this posture. They trusted me then, and they still trust me now, because they never had to wonder what was happening behind closed doors.

Transparency wasn't a tactic. It was a way of leading. It said, "You are part of this story. You're not just here to execute decisions. You deserve to see them, understand them, and carry them with me."

Closing, Why Culture Held

Looking back, I don't see these decisions as extras. They were the culture. Daily rhythms that kept us aligned. MWI Cares reminded people they weren't alone. The 80/20 rule gave margin for growth. Health and wellness that valued the whole person. Transparency that left no doubt about trust.

None of these practices was glamorous. They didn't make headlines. But they became the strength of our team. They made it possible for people to thrive, not just produce. They created a foundation we would need when the harder seasons came.

Culture isn't built in crisis. It's revealed there. And because we built it here, when the weight showed up later, in moments of grief, conflict, and strain, we weren't crushed by it. The culture held.

Chapter 6

The Cost of the Climb

The Drift Beneath the Wins

2019 through 2021 should have been the years of steady ascent. We were winning business, doing good work, and the world's reliance on technology only deepened during the pandemic. For most companies like ours, it was the perfect storm of demand. But while the charts and numbers looked right, something underneath began to fracture.

Our town never really saw the pandemic the way the news made it sound. Life kept moving, but fear still ruled the day. Everywhere you turned, people were uncertain whether their businesses or jobs would survive. Years of fear-based messaging trained people to look inward and protect their own. That crevasse we now see between employees and "the man" widened quickly during this season. The data backs it up: surveys from 2020–2021 showed steep declines in employee trust of leadership and a surge in expectations that companies should prove they cared about people, not just profits. The "self-first" mindset had momentum, and it created chaos inside and outside the business.

I noticed the cracks most clearly in myself. I had always been deeply connected to the rhythms of our work, from client meetings to team culture to how we showed up in the community. I knew the beat of our company like a musician knows the tempo of a song. But during those years, the pressure and pace of the season pulled me away from the forward-facing side of the business almost overnight.

One moment stands out. We had delivered strong work for a client for years. When their own team created a mess, I called it out directly and fairly. Their leader didn't like that. He pulled us into a meeting, forcing us to drive forty minutes each way without an agenda, and blamed me for their mistakes before firing us in a very disrespectful way. I didn't mind being fired, I knew the work had been excellent. What bothered me was the absence of care. I expected someone to stand shoulder to shoulder with me in that moment. Instead, silence. It took days before I heard a word. Something broke then. It wasn't just about losing a client. It was the moment I recognized, more clearly than ever, that when relational fallout hit, I was still the one expected to absorb it, and the silence around me simply confirmed what had already been true for years.

That fracture left me less visible on the outside, but it pushed me deeper into what I loved most: serving my people. I poured myself into the team. My energy went toward creating stability in a season when fear and division were everywhere. In a way, that shift planted the seed for this book. After the sale, I would go from leading everything to leading very little. But here, I was still in the fight, still protecting what mattered.

Cracks in the Foundation

Not every loss was abstract. Some cut deep. I remember a meeting where we debated new maternity and paternity leave policies. The conversation turned toward replacing the words "mother" and "father" with "birthing person." I couldn't go there. For me, that moment highlighted a tension I felt growing inside myself, a sense that what mattered most to me in leadership no longer aligned with the direction some conversations were beginning to take.

Another wound came when my marketing team was reassigned. I had handpicked them, sharp, teachable, passionate young women who gave everything and more. Watching them thrive was one of my greatest joys. When restructuring moved them under different leadership, it hit harder than I expected. They weren't just colleagues; they were an extension of me.

Looking back, the cracks weren't dramatic explosions. They were quiet shifts, in language, in decisions, in how people were treated. But leadership is sensitive to the subtle. A song only needs to lose tempo by a beat or two before the whole band feels off.

Pocket rule: Revenue without relationship is erosion.

Lineage callout: This was Sinek's truth in motion. Profit is a result, not a purpose.

The cracks that started beneath the surface didn't stay hidden for long. They grew into patterns I couldn't ignore. What had once been a culture built on care and trust began to feel the pull of increasing demands, more projects, more expectations, more urgency. On paper, it looked like maturity, bigger projects, more revenue, and new policies. But underneath, it felt hollow.

Culture rarely changes with one big decision. It shifts in the small things: a word chosen in a meeting, a policy written without heart, a client taken on because the pace of the moment made it easier to say yes than to slow down and evaluate the fit. One by one, those decisions stacked until the tone of the business was different.

I had always believed that growth and care could coexist. In fact, that was the foundation of servant leadership. But I started to see that the two don't live in balance by accident. If you don't fight for care, growth will smother it. Fear accelerates the drift. With the world shouting about survival, the pressures around us pulled the culture toward revenue as if it were the only proof of life.

I felt the weight of it most in the way people carried themselves. Conversations with staff that once felt open and energized now felt guarded. Huddles and rhythms that used to breathe life into the team started to feel like obligations. People still worked hard, but you could sense the atmosphere tightening. It was as if the pace of the season made everyone brace for evaluation rather than connection.

This is what Robert Greenleaf meant when he wrote about stewardship, a concept he pioneered as the father of modern servant leadership. Leaders aren't just responsible for producing results; they're responsible for how those results are achieved and what happens to people in the process. A company can win contracts and still lose its soul.

Pocket rule: Culture doesn't collapse overnight, it drifts degree by degree until no one recognizes the room they're in.

The business was still functioning. We weren't falling apart, but the pace was relentless. As the workload intensified, the choices being made naturally leaned toward speed and efficiency, and people were asked to give more than they had. They delivered, but you could see the wear setting in.

So I turned inward, back to what I could still protect.

Carrying What's Left

In that climate, I found myself leaning harder into care. Not as a hero swooping in, just as a leader refusing to forget the human side when the current pulled the other way. I paid closer attention to how people were doing, not just what they were producing. I reminded them they weren't invisible. I tried to steady the room when the pressure around us kept rising.

This was the same season I was asked to investigate a struggling designer, with the quiet assumption that I'd return recommending termination. Instead, we ended up on the crying couch. What looked like performance issues turned out to be the weight of personal struggle. That conversation didn't just save a job; it reminded me why I leaned harder into care when everything else was growing cold.

But it took something out of me too. Years of leadership had already left their mark, and this was different. Carrying the weight of culture drift, of watching good people slowly get used up, left me drained. The fatigue wasn't only physical. It was emotional and spiritual, the kind that lingers long after you leave the office.

Leadership at its best is about multiplying strength. Leadership at its costliest is about carrying tension that never seems to resolve. I was living in that space.

That space had limits I hadn't named yet.

Pocket rule: Care is clearest when everything else grows cold.

The Debt Comes Due

Every leader has a threshold, though most of us don't see it until we're already standing on the edge. For me, the years of 2019–2021 brought me to mine. The business was still moving, but inside I was wearing down.

I could feel it in my body first. The pace wasn't slowing, and neither was the pressure. My health began to decline faster than I could recover. Fatigue became my constant companion. Nights stretched long with little sleep. Even the simplest decisions started carrying more weight than they should have.

Spiritually, I was running on fumes. The joy that had carried me through the early years, the belief that servant leadership could transform not only a company but the people inside it, felt distant. I wasn't doubting the principle. I was doubting whether I had the capacity to keep living in a culture that no longer made space for it.

The breaking point wasn't one dramatic moment. It was a slow recognition: if I kept going this way, something would give. Either my health would collapse, or I would lose myself trying to keep the team from being consumed by the climb.

That's when I realized survival isn't always about pushing through. Sometimes survival is about stepping back before the cost becomes too great.

Pocket rule: Culture debt always comes due. And leaders often pay it first.

Looking back, the climb didn't break the company, it broke me. On the outside, we were still delivering, still growing, still telling the story of success. But on the inside, I was exhausted, running out of margin in every direction.

What made this season dangerous wasn't the workload. It was how quietly the strain blended into normal operations. Meetings still happened. Metrics still moved. From the outside, very little looked broken. But the distance between what the organization needed and what I could sustainably give was growing, and I hadn't named it yet.

What I lost in those years was not my belief in servant leadership. If anything, the opposite happened. I became more convinced than ever that people matter more than numbers, and that when values drift, leaders and teams pay the price. What I lost was my capacity to keep absorbing the strain inside a system that no longer aligned with who I was.

That bill had come due, and I carried more of it than I could afford.

Pocket rule: Leadership isn't free. If you don't set the terms of the cost, it will set them for you.

That emptiness, that imbalance, would follow me into Midwestern Built (MWB). The same exhaustion that hollowed me out at MWI was waiting on the other side, only this time it wasn't a warning. It was a reality I couldn't escape. My life was closing in on me, and it would continue to do so for far too long.

I helped found Midwestern Built as an investor in a friend's dream back in 2016. My part was capital, counsel, and guardrails, just as far as he'd let me. I wasn't the operator; I was the quiet partner financing and advising from the sidelines. For years it stayed in the background while I ran Midwestern Interactive, but that early partnership would later test everything I believed about stewardship and trust.

Chapter 7

The Bridge

The Sale

July 1, 2022, was supposed to feel like a triumph. In many ways, it did.

I had built something over the course of a thirty-year career that held enough value to give me a long, well-funded runway into whatever came next. For the first time in my life, I had margin. I could breathe financially. I was able to help my kids in ways that mattered, not just token gifts, but significant steps forward for their lives.

I bought my mom a van. It was a thank-you for the life she and my father had given me when they adopted me as an infant. I gave generously to our church. I did the things I had always hoped success would let me do. On the outside, it looked like I was living my best life, and in many ways, I was.

But on the inside, I was crushed.

Some of the people I had spent years in the trenches with, people who had shared boardrooms, deadlines, and vision-casting sessions with me, began to treat my presence as optional. Whether they hated me or not wasn't the point. What became clear was that as my role shifted from partner to COO, the space I once occupied in the room shifted too.

That dissonance nearly tore me in two. Outwardly, I was thriving. Inwardly, I was grieving.

Pocket rule: Wealth can widen your reach, but it can't fill the silence of being unwanted.

The Silence

I had nine days.

That was it, nine days where I thought maybe, just maybe, this might work out. Nine days of waking up without the crushing schedule, without the endless crises, without the pressure to carry more than was human. Nine days of thinking there might finally be space for rest, for health, for something resembling balance.

July 9, 2022, it was gone.

Nine days of breathing room turned into "all in" on the next mess. Screw being healthy. Screw resting. The bridge I thought might be space to recover became nothing more than a handoff into another battle.

That season taught me something about servant leadership I hadn't seen as clearly before: in power-driven environments, kindness is often misunderstood, not because it's weak, but because it asks more of a leader than dominance ever will. I had chosen the noble way out at MWI. I hadn't fought for scraps of authority. I had let go with dignity. But in the eyes of others, that restraint looked like permission. It was easy to treat it like permission.

Pocket rule: Servant leadership is not submission, it is sacrifice with strength intact.

I wasn't weak. I had always led by giving people the benefit of the doubt. That's the reflex of a servant leader. You assume the best. You extend grace. You trust first. But there comes a time when grace has to be paired with grit, when the role of a servant leader isn't to absorb, but to act.

Pocket rule: Sometimes the kindest thing a leader can do is draw a hard line.

The stillness after MWI wasn't rest. It was the moment before another storm.

The Hollow Role

I never needed power or authority. Ego wasn't what drove me. What mattered was having a voice, a seat at the table where culture was shaped and people were protected.

When I sat down at my desk for the first time as COO in mid-August, I looked out my window and saw activity buzzing through the office. The company was moving forward, but without me. In just forty-five days, it hadn't only moved on; it had begun to reject my way of leading altogether.

Within just a couple of weeks, that became clearest in one meeting I'll never forget. I didn't ask to be there. In fact, the only reason I was in the room was that other leaders didn't want to be. They avoided the confrontation, and it landed in my lap by default. It was token, patronizing, likely with the expectation that I'd do what I eventually did: walk away.

The conversation turned toward "birthing people." Maybe that kind of ideology had been simmering just under the surface all along, but hearing it spoken as the new language of the company broke something in me. I watched as women and mothers, roles I believe carry a God-given significance in a healthy society, were reduced by sterile terminology. It wasn't just about words. Words were the doorway to action, and the goal was to strip dignity from both.

Sitting there, I realized that even if I had wanted to push back, my ability to lead had already been stripped of any real impact. To raise my voice would have meant war, and I no longer had the authority to fight one.

Pocket rule: When leaders avoid the hard things, they leave others to carry wounds they won't even claim.

It was a hurtful, empty place to sit, watching a culture I had poured my life into slide away, while knowing I no longer had the strength or the standing to call it back.

Aftershock

By October 2022, I had officially stepped away from MWI. I told myself it was the right thing to do, dignified, necessary, even healthy. But grief doesn't operate on a schedule.

The aftershock hit in November.

I was sitting on a plane bound for Arizona, ready for a CrossFit competition, when my phone buzzed. On the other end came the news: three of my closest team members, the marketing team I had personally hired, mentored, and fought for, had been terminated without warning.

There was nowhere to go, nowhere to hide. My head hit my hands. The tears came. Right there in public, on that plane, I felt helpless.

The sting ran deeper because the shift hadn't been sudden. A year earlier, I had seen that team reassigned in a way that troubled me. They were placed under someone whose strengths weren't centered on leading people, and the transition signaled a shift in priorities I couldn't ignore. In that moment, culture felt secondary to direction, and the change revealed how differently leadership value was being interpreted across the organization.

So when the call came, it wasn't just the shock of their departure. It was the final blow in a story I had already watched unfold in slow motion.

But my response afterward was the only kind I knew how to give: I helped them land on their feet. Carie and I threw our weight behind them. We worked our networks, opened doors, and celebrated each win. And one by one, they found jobs that fit them. Every single one landed well.

Pocket rule: If you can't protect people where they are, then you fight to send them somewhere they'll thrive.

The Weight I Carried

By December, the full weight of the gym had landed squarely on my shoulders. There was no cushion, no buffer, no team of executives to share the load. It was me.

And the weight wasn't one-dimensional.

On one side was survival. The mortgage had to be paid. Payroll was non-negotiable. Equipment, utilities, insurance, the bills didn't care about culture; they demanded cash. From July of 2022 until March of 2025, we were losing between eight and ten thousand dollars every single month. I know that number because I wrote the check. Thirty-four months in a row. Each one carving away a little more of my margin, my reserves, my strength.

By this point, I was the sole leader of the gym. Every decision, every conflict, and every pressure in this season belonged to me alone.

It wasn't just the math. It was the dysfunction piled on top of it, decisions that made no sense, energy wasted in conflict instead of building, constant fires that drained more than they produced. The weight wasn't only financial; it was cultural.

And all of it was pressing down on me at a time when my own health was already in decline. My body had been sending warning signals for years, but now they were impossible to ignore. The pressure made every symptom worse. Some days it felt like leadership had turned into a deadly game, and I was the only one left at the table. Maybe that sounds like an overstatement. But it's not far from the truth I was living.

On the other side was something even more important to me: people. From the beginning, I had believed a gym should be more than a place to sweat. It should be a place where anyone, any age, gender, fitness level, or background, could find belonging and success. That vision wasn't optional. It was the soul of the place. And if it was going to survive, that soul had to be protected.

So I carried both sides, the spreadsheets and the spirit.

Some days it felt like trying to lift with one arm strapped behind my back. Some days it felt like a fight I couldn't win. But I kept showing up, because the alternative was to let it all burn.

Pocket rule: Sometimes the heaviest weight a leader carries isn't the numbers; it's the people who will be crushed if the numbers win.

The bridge wasn't a pause. It wasn't a chance to rest. It was a crucible, a place where everything I had left was tested.

Lineage callout: This was Greenleaf's "stewardship" under fire, the test of whether I would protect both the mission and the people, even when it cost me everything.

Chapter 8

The Fire After the Fall

The Turning Point

December 2022 brought more loss.

Within six months, I had been forced to let go of one company I built and then found myself holding the full weight of another. First, MWI slipped from my hands. Then MWB shifted entirely onto my shoulders.

The circumstances didn't matter as much as the reality: if Midwestern Built was going to survive, it was up to me. There was no backup plan, no one else to steady the load. The business was bleeding money, and the culture wasn't fragile, it was broken into a thousand pieces.

So I did what I had always done: I stepped in. I shouldered the weight no one else was willing to carry. Not because it was easy. Not because it made financial sense. But because there were members and coaches who deserved a place worth fighting for.

There is a moment in every crisis when you watch the exit door swing open and decide to stay anyway. For me, that moment didn't happen in a boardroom. It happened on an ordinary weekday, standing by the whiteboard as classes changed over. A mom who had been away for months walked back in, nervous and quiet. A retiree taped his wrist and smiled like he was home. A young guy asked for the bar with less knurling because his hands tore easily. No speeches. Just people choosing to keep going. I could leave. Or I could stand where I said I would.

Pocket rule: Servant leadership doesn't fixate on what's gone, it protects what remains.

Survival Mode

The math was brutal. From July of 2022 until March of 2025, we were losing between eight and ten thousand dollars every month. Thirty-four months in a row. I know because I wrote the checks.

This wasn't an abstract number on a spreadsheet. It was money pulled directly from my personal reserves, poured into keeping the gym alive. Payroll. Mortgage. Utilities. Insurance. Every line item demanded cash, and there was no "pause" button. The gym had to run, even when the numbers screamed otherwise. When equipment failed, it wasn't a theoretical expense, it was an immediate decision between repair now or bigger problems later. When a vendor bill hit, it didn't care how tired I was. When the insurance was renewed, it didn't check our feelings about the last quarter.

Every month felt like stepping into a ring, knowing I'd get hit, hoping I'd still be standing when the bell rang, and then doing it all over again thirty-three more times. That isn't drama. It's arithmetic.

Carie carried it with me. I worked the math with our accountant, bookkeeper, and investment advisor, line by line, month after month. The checks still came from us, but the decisions were made with counsel and data, not late-night panic. We cut what didn't serve the mission. We paid for what protected people. We delayed what could wait without hurting members or staff. It was unglamorous stewardship, no ribbon-cuttings, no "look at us" posts. Just choices that kept the floor safe and the doors open.

There was also a necessary stopgap I had to end. A monthly "guaranteed payment" had been baked into expectations. Maybe that made sense once. In a business running this far in the red, it made no sense at all. A company cannot guarantee distributions it cannot afford. Ending it wasn't aggression. It was owning the responsibility.

Pocket rule: A leader's sacrifice is invisible until the checks stop clearing.

It would have been easier to walk away, to let the business collapse under its own weight. But walking away would have meant more than losing money. It would have meant abandoning people. And that I could not do.

Cultural Defense

From the beginning, my vision for Midwestern Built was never just about fitness. It was about people. It was about creating a place where anyone, any age, gender, fitness level, or background, could belong and succeed.

But in that season, the vision that had driven us from the start felt buried under the sheer weight of strain. Conversations about the state of the business were strained and scattered, often shaped more by the pressure of the moment than by the clarity we all needed. In times of pressure, any organization can drift toward metrics, urgency, and survival mode, treating members as numbers, coaches as operators, and culture as something that can be rebuilt later. The danger is that even well-intentioned teams can slip into that pattern without noticing. For a stretch of time, that was the current we were trying to fight our way through.

I couldn't let that happen.

So I showed up every day, not just to pay the bills, but to protect the soul of the gym. The strain of the season had created currents that pulled people in different directions, and my work was to steady the middle. I focused on supporting coaches when the pressure around us made the room feel heavy. I fought to preserve an environment where members didn't just come to work out, but to heal, grow, and belong.

Basic things mattered again: classes starting on time; warm-ups that prepared people, not just filled minutes; whiteboard briefs that sounded like an invitation, not a test. It wasn't glamorous leadership. There were no press releases, no applause. It was daily defense. It was absorbing blows so others didn't have to.

I also changed the way we communicated. By the time I stepped into full responsibility, communication had become fragmented, and people were filling gaps with whatever information they could find. I corrected that. In those first months, I wrote often, emails to members, notes on social channels, short and direct: what was changing, why it was changing, and what people could count on. I wasn't trying to win an argument. I was building trust. Questions went up at first, as they should. But the volume of rumors went down. Clarity does that.

And I kept the center in view, the middle of the room where everyone lives. Progress was small and ordinary: people returning after setbacks, relearning movements, and showing up when life was heavy. No highlight reel, just steady work. That was the point.

Pocket rule: Protect the culture, even when it costs you personally.

The Personal Toll

Protection came at a price.

My health had already been in decline during the last years at MWI. Stress, poor sleep, and constant sacrifice took their toll. By the time I stepped into MWB full-time, my tank was already empty. The weight of the financial bleed, the dysfunction, and the cultural defense pushed me even further. Nights grew shorter. Blood pressure climbed. My body protested in ways I couldn't ignore.

Leadership at that point wasn't inspiring or energizing. It was survival. I showed up because I had to, not because I felt strong enough to. That kind of honesty isn't heroic. It's necessary. You can pretend your capacity is infinite, but your body will correct you.

I started listening. The doctor told me to throttle back. The counselor handed me practical tools: slow the inputs; take walks before screens; lift four to six days a week; eat like you want to keep the body God gave you; write down what you're carrying so it doesn't own your head. None of that was performance. It was stewardship. Exhausted leaders make expensive mistakes.

So I acted like I believed it. Simple meals. Earlier nights. Scripture opens before inboxes. Walks without a phone. Short workouts that didn't require adrenaline to count. Not dramatic. Sustainable. My resting heart rate started to drift down. The edges of my patience came back. I wasn't "better." I was at least pointed in the right direction.

There's a difference between the kind of fire that refines and the kind that consumes. For much of my career, the fire had refined me. It had sharpened resilience, clarified convictions, and forged leadership. But here, the fire wanted to consume. The only way through was to lower the flames, not by quitting, but by refusing to feed them.

Pocket rule: Servant leadership doesn't guarantee health for the leader. Sometimes it demands it.

Fighting Back

I've always led by giving people the benefit of the doubt. That reflex, assume the best, extend grace, trust first, didn't change. But inside the gym, that grace was misread as weakness.

In a meeting with several witnesses, something was said that clarified a deeper misalignment: the priorities in the room no longer felt aligned around shared responsibility. In that moment, the relationship shifted. I was no longer being engaged as a teammate, but as a resource. At the same time, I was already covering losses and financing survival, and the expectation was that I would continue doing so to support someone else's next ascent.

That posture runs counter to servant leadership. When the mission is bleeding, a servant leader protects the whole so the people inside it can endure. Personal advancement comes after collective stability—not before it. When the team is cared for, progress follows.

Staying servant-led didn't mean passivity. It meant stewardship with a spine: no guaranteed payouts while the business bled; no terms that put an individual ahead of the mission; no decisions that elevated self-interest over collective health. I gathered proofs, moved through the process, and acted—not for ego or control, but for the people the gym existed to serve.

There were days it felt like I was wasting breath. Then a small signal would show up, a class that ran clean, a coach who felt backed even when we disagreed privately, a member who stayed after to say, "This feels like it used to." Those were markers on the trail. Not victory laps. Directional signs.

Pocket rule: Servant leaders carry towels, not doormats. Lineage callout: This was Greenleaf's stewardship in practice, protecting both mission and people, even when it cost me.

The Handoff

By October 2023, the other side had engaged counsel. I retained counsel I trusted, chose silence as discipline, and kept showing up. Stewardship, not spectacle. Negotiations surface priorities you can't see until the process forces them into daylight. We would carry the fire only as long as it protected people, and then we would pass it with dignity.

I didn't need to be the closer. I needed to be faithful. That meant finishing the part of the work that still belonged to me, and refusing to grab what didn't.

The months that followed were heavy but clear. The bridge had to be built before it could be crossed.

The next chapter tells how we crossed that bridge.

Chapter 9

The Bridge

Silence on Purpose

From late July until late October of 2023, I couldn't step into the gym I owned seventy-five percent of. The process required distance, and I stayed locked in on the goal. Attorneys carried the communication. My job was to stay disciplined and let the process play out.

So I went quiet on purpose. I dug deeper into the numbers. I listened when people came with questions and concerns, but I only answered what I could confirm. Anything else, I left alone. Silence wasn't withdrawal, it was stewardship. It was giving the process time to do its work without adding more sparks.

Behind the scenes, I kept preparing. Dissolution was coming, and I was going to be ready the moment it was complete. Quiet work. Careful listening. No noise. Not everything deserves your voice, especially when your voice is what the room is watching.

Taking the Weight

In November 2023, the separation was completed, and I became the sole owner of both gyms. Walking in felt like moving into a house that was familiar, but carried a presence that needed some cultural elbow grease. We'd been losing eight to ten thousand dollars a month since mid-2022. Carie and I had been covering the gap to keep the doors open. Now the weight sat squarely on me.

Day one wasn't a speech; it was a sweep. I walked the floor and touched the details that tell the truth: scuffed plyo boxes, a whiteboard with three different handwriting styles, and a stack of rubber plates still warm from the morning class. The heaters hummed; the room felt tired. I pulled a rower out of a traffic lane, reset the chalk bucket where people actually grip, checked the bike batteries, and tossed two cracked 35-pound plates. None of that wins a marketing award. It tells a room, "someone's paying attention again."

Carthage was steadier; Brock led it well. Joplin was thin, membership down, trust thin, a gravitational pull toward "elite" that made ordinary members feel like renters. I didn't broadcast a turnaround plan. I reset the center: members first, coaches second, me last. Simple doesn't mean easy; it means no excuses.

The first thirty days were about oxygen. Fix the air the room breathes: predictable class times, a warm-up that prepares rather than fills, coaches backed in public so the floor feels safe. The next thirty days were about friction. Move what people trip over, literally and culturally. The third thirty days were about stamina. Could we keep this cadence without flaring out? If servant leadership works, it should scale to Tuesday at 3 p.m., not just launch days and announcements.

I converted the office into a lounge. Not décor, a message. This was a place anyone could gather. No closed door unless absolutely necessary. If I had administrative work, I did it off-site. In the building, my job was presence: shake hands, learn names, spot friction before it turns into fallout, listen more than I speak. Presence isn't a mood; it's policy. It says, you matter more than my calendar.

Resetting the Center

Transparency hadn't been the norm. People learned in the dark and repeated what they didn't know. I flipped it. Early on, I wrote often, not-so-short notes to members about what was changing, why, and what they could count on; quick messages to coaches about expectations and support. I wasn't trying to win an argument. I was building trust. Questions went up at first, and rumor volume went down. Clarity does that.

I asked a handful of men I trust to hold me to the mission. No standing meetings. On-demand by text and email, short, direct, honest. This board's job wasn't to run the business; it was to keep me inside guardrails when compromise looked clever. If a decision was major, I brought them in. That isn't a weakness. It's how you keep leadership from drifting into self-service.

Repair shows up in small signals before it shows up in numbers. Fewer flare-ups at the whiteboard. Direct messages that ask, "Can we talk?" instead of "I'm done." A new member who lingers after class because the coach remembered their kid's name. A veteran who quietly helps a first-timer with a collar and then fades back into the group. No hashtags. Just health.

I kept my own rhythms honest. The redline I'd lived at since 2021 didn't vanish just because I held new responsibilities. I began training four to six days a week, Carie was helping me eat better, opened Scripture before inboxes, and slept like I wanted to keep this body. None of that was performance. It was stewardship. Exhausted leaders make expensive mistakes.

Culture heals faster when problems are addressed without becoming the center of the culture. I refused to turn dysfunction into a story. No casting. No audience. Repair over theater. That meant shutting down public crossfire and moving hard conversations into quiet rooms. Defend leaders in public; disagree in private. Reward trust—not volume.

Standards on the Floor

Our coaches already knew how to coach. I didn't need to script progressions or argue rep schemes. My part was the standard and the environment.

The whiteboard is presented as the best opportunity of the day, with no side commentary or live undercutting. If there's disagreement, we handle it offline like adults. The coach owns the floor during class. Class comes first, even when someone's training solo nearby. Respect for the room is shared. Coaches manage the flow and the noise, and members match that respect. During the briefing, setups pause or stay quiet, no clanging plates, no bar drops, and open-gym athletes and coaches go silent while the coach communicates.

That sounded simple on paper and complex in practice. We were unwinding learned habits: setting up personal equipment during the brief because "that's how we've always done it," dropping plates that covered up important communication, whispering side coaching during someone else's hour, and open-gym workouts that bled into class time. None of this was malicious. It was entropy. Setting new standards is how you reverse it.

This matters beyond a gym. In any business, there's a "floor", the moment where your customer faces your craft. In that moment, the professional owns the environment. You can't deliver clarity to the people you serve if the room won't hold still long enough for them to hear. Respect for the room is respect for the person you're serving.

Team over talent was the next layer. The hat you wear inside the gym is coach, not competitor. Present one plan in public; bring disagreement to the table, not the floor. Some embraced that; some didn't. When local collaboration on programming stalled, I tested a third-party plan. It looked great on paper and landed wrong for our people. I put programming back with the steward whose work matched our values and served the whole room. Sometimes the path to change proves that change wasn't necessary.

Price Follows Service

The decision I dreaded most was price. For years, our rates lagged what the market would bear. We had room to increase. The question wasn't "can we," it was "should we, and when." My answer stays the same: price follows service. It comes last, after the value is visible in the room.

I took the question to the board that holds me to the mission. We didn't argue feelings. We walked the logic like adults, service first, price last, access protected. They pushed where I was soft and trimmed where I was sentimental. We kept a scholarship lane, invited local sponsorships, tightened the member note, and set a review date so the decision wouldn't be "set and forget." Guardrails, not theater.

We rolled it out with notice and with help, not surprise and spin. I owned the decision. I owned the timing. I owned the promise behind it: if we ask more, we deliver more. And if someone needed a bridge, we would build one. Price is not a trophy. It's a tool.

Progress didn't look like a victory lap. It looked like steadier classes, fewer rumor-fueled blowups, faster answers, and less whiplash. First-timers didn't feel like intruders. Veterans didn't feel like babysitters. Programming conversations settled because identity settled first. We were still carrying the cost. We were still cleaning up after decisions that predated my return. Fine. Cost wasn't the measure. Integrity was. Do the next right thing at the right pace with the right guardrails, and keep showing up when you're tired.

The Handoff

In late October 2024, Carie and I sat with our financial advisor. The cash burn was crushing our future. We made a simple, hard call: eight more months. If the business didn't turn by then, we would sell or shut it down.

In early November 2024, a message landed from Mica, who owned another gym in town: would we consider selling? I wasn't ready, but it read like an answer to a quiet prayer. I brought it to the board. They agreed, unanimously. We started negotiations. They ran through March 2025. It wasn't easy. There were normal complexities that made it take longer than expected. We stayed with the process and finished.

By early 2025, it was clear I wasn't rebuilding to stay. Months earlier, Carie and I had already decided to give the gym eight more months to turn around before we'd have to sell or shut it down. I was building a bridge. My job wasn't to prove I could hold the reins forever; it was to deliver something survivable to the next steward.

One Thursday in January, the gym was quiet, the kind of quiet that lets truth surface. The sale terms were mapped. I walked the perimeter one more time like a landlord checking outlets, rig bolts tight, rowers straight, med balls where a new member wouldn't feel in the way. No music. No audience. I wasn't rehearsing a goodbye; I was finishing a promise.

The sale was finalized in March 2025. No confetti. No speech. I signed, shook hands, and walked to the door. I was tired. I was at peace, the kind of peace you get when you keep promises other people can't verify but you. We protected the center. We reset standards. We told the truth early. We used process over performance. We priced last, and only after the service led. We refused to feed the drama. We finished with dignity and ended with clarity.

Bridges don't get spotlights. They get people safely across. That's enough.

Chapter 10

The Rise of Archetype

I didn't get relief; I got room to breathe. Not in Joplin, in Carthage. The sale closed one story there; the work changed shape here. No victory lap. No speech. Just a little space back.

The name on the wall was next. Midwestern Built had carried us for years, but it no longer told the truth about the gym, or about me. We didn't try to rescue it. We laid it down and set a standard that matched how we were actually living. For a long stretch my work had been wrapped in "Midwestern", first software, then strength. Same intent: lead well and build something that matters. Same lesson: the cost is real. Letting go wasn't administrative; it was personal. I designed that brand. I cared about it. But we needed a clean standard, not just a fresh coat of paint. So we raised a new banner: Archetype Fitness Company.

People who loved Midwestern Built will remember it; I honor that. But the name we carry now has to match the standard we were going to start living, again.

Pocket rule: Standards change cultures; names reveal them.

Archetype: returning to the pattern

Archetype means the original pattern, the thing you build from, not a copy you chase. That was the point: stop compensating, start telling the truth about who we are.

Plain terms: we're a class-based gym in Carthage. Leaders and coaches design programs that serve every level, first-timers and veterans in the same room, each with a way forward. Body and mind strengthen each other. Structure matters. So does the challenge. Community shapes outcomes. Respect first. Encouragement in the open. Accountability without theater. A room that's safe to fail in becomes a room where people try harder things.

We believe people are made in the image of God. That conviction sits under how we lead: serve first, tell the truth, protect dignity, keep access wide, and build something that outlives us. We don't press that belief onto anyone. We refuse to separate it from our story.

Mission, simple enough for a wall, strong enough for a Tuesday at 3 p.m.: help people get better, body, mind, and spirit.

The phoenix became our mark, not because it's clever but because it's honest. Everyone faces fire, illness, doubt, loss, and failure. Rising isn't pretending the fire didn't happen. It's rebuilding afterward, stronger, steadier, with people around you who care if you make it. There's a resurrection echo in that for me. I won't pretend otherwise.

When we shared the rebrand with core Carthage members, the people who quietly held the place together, the room didn't cheer; it settled. Heads nodded. Tense shoulders dropped. The questions were right: Will programming still serve every level? Will events keep the same heart? Will this invite more people in or push them out? My answer was steady: we aren't erasing our past; we're naming what you already feel. "Archetype" fit the room. Within days, the new name showed up where it mattered, on apparel, in text threads, in the way folks invited their friends. Oxygen.

Not my dream, still my duty

The gym wasn't my dream. I started as a member and investor. I'm not a fitness expert; I'm an owner who cares about people and systems. Archetype is me holding the center long enough for the one with the dream, Brock, to fully step into it.

Servant leadership looks like that more often than we admit. Sometimes you take ownership of something you're not passionate about because you are passionate about the people it connects you to. You carry what isn't "your thing" so someone else can do their thing. You flatten the road so the next steward can run harder. You don't need a spotlight to carry the moment; you need standards that protect people while the work matures.

That posture changed how I showed up. In Joplin I lived on the floor, present, absorbing, guarding. In Carthage I could train first and steward always. I still shook hands, said thanks, and watched edges, but there wasn't a daily fire to put out. A healthier culture changes a leader's job description: fewer interventions, more formation.

How Archetype actually works

Carthage had been mostly healthy for years and was largely insulated from what plagued Joplin. It had its own share of challenges, but it was always very interesting to me how different the community was. They chose to stand together rather than be blown apart. Brock runs the day-to-day clean: steady classes, clear expectations, attention on humans before numbers. My role sits upstream, owns the standard, keeps the guardrails, protects the mission, and makes the calls that outlive any single class.

What that means in practice:

- People & trust. We select coaches who can lead the room and protect dignity at the same time. We defend them in public and coach them in private. When a seam pops, we fix it now, not after a season.

- Respect the room. Whiteboard means quiet, no bar-drop punctuation, no side programming drowning out the coach. Members aren't props; they're the point. That expectation translates to any business: protect the moment where your work meets the person you serve.

- Access without drift. The scholarship lane stays open. Money shouldn't lock out people who belong here. We invite sponsorships that widen access without bending values.

- Clear lanes. Coaches own the craft. Leaders own the context. Owners own the standard. Crossing those lines creates noise; staying in them creates trust.

- Accountability without theater. A small board of voices tells me the truth. No standing meetings. Short notes when decisions are big, move, risk, guardrail. Their job isn't to run the gym; it's to keep me honest when compromise looks clever.

- Communication with a center. We say the quiet parts early, what's changing, why it's changing, and what members can count on. Less mystique, more clarity. Clarity beats drama every time.

A word on programming. We keep it for every level. Not watered down, scaled. Strength cycles are written with on-ramps and off-ramps. Conditioning blocks are built to challenge without humiliating anyone into silence. You can work hard without auditioning. That's a moral choice as much as a coaching one.

A word on events. We still mark seasons, intramural throwdowns, simple benchmarks, and bring-a-friend days. But none of it overshadows the daily class. Tuesday matters more than Saturday. Ordinary days are where people change.

A word on coaching culture. Coaches aren't celebrities. They're stewards. We expect them to know names, watch movement, and speak to the person in front of them, not to their own ambitions. If you've got a competitive goal, great, pursue it. In class, your first job is to serve the room.

Years on a soundboard formed that posture in me: signal over spotlight. The job isn't to be the loudest voice; it's to make sure the right things are heard and the wrong noise doesn't win.

Pocket rule: Own the standard; free the operators.

Faith in plain sight

We don't turn classes into services. We also don't hide our center. The Imago Dei conviction shows up in practical ways: how we correct without shaming; why we keep access wide; how we handle conflict (direct, private, honest); what we celebrate (effort and integrity before times and totals). It shows up in the way we talk about bodies, with gratitude, not contempt. And it shows up when someone hits a wall and needs more than a scaling option, they need a human to sit with them for a minute and remind them that starting again is still starting.

We keep the door open for anyone. We refuse to apologize for the values that make the place safe. That's not culture war. That's culture care.

More than a membership

We say this out loud: fitness is more than a membership, it's a mission. The mission doesn't stop at our doors. Some people won't join our classes. We still serve them.

That looks like:

- Simple on-ramps for people starting over, no shame, clear steps, a coach who remembers your name next time.

- Community sessions anyone can attend, move, learn, and ask basic questions without feeling exposed.

- Content that teaches families how to move and eat without extremes. No magic. No hacks. Just patient work.

- Bridge helps when a member hits a financial pothole. Quiet, targeted, accountable. Dignity intact.

- Partnerships with local orgs to host lift-and-learn nights or wellness basics for teams who've never felt welcome in a gym.

None of that makes us famous. It makes us useful.

Outside the walls, my work has space again. I'm mentoring and consulting, quiet, targeted help where I can add clarity without taking a seat that isn't mine. A nonprofit needs processes so passion doesn't cannibalize the mission. A trades company wants a hiring flow that protects culture without gatekeeping talent. A pastor asks how to rebuild elder accountability without burning the church down. These aren't "gigs." They're extensions of the same conviction: guardrails set people free.

Rebuilding the builder

Two things had to be rebuilt after the sale: the gym's name and me. I never measured health with bravado. I measure it by basic obedience: am I keeping promises? Am I telling the truth? Am I sleeping? Am I training four to six days a week without making it a penance? Am I eating in a way that supports life, not control? Am I honoring Carie with time and attention that isn't spent? Am I limiting the adrenaline habits I picked up when everything felt like a fight?

Some days I do that well. Some days I do it clumsily. But I do it. That slow rebuild is part of Archetype's honest story: the room is for people, including the guy who owns the building.

Peace is coming back the way exhaustion arrived, quietly. You notice it when an email doesn't make you flinch. When you sleep and actually recover. When thirty minutes under a barbell doesn't require adrenaline to count. When a coach corrects a miss without defensiveness. When a member says, "I brought a friend because it feels safe here."

I don't confuse peace with arrival. It's a green light: keep going. Fewer public battles, more private repair. Fewer declarations, more decisions. Less "watch me," more "let me watch you do it."

That's the part of my story I can tell and I'm sticking to it.

Chapter 11

Introduction to the Fundamentals

Part One of this book was about the fire. The crossings. The weight of what leadership cost me, and the reality of what it gave back. I told you stories, some raw, some still tender, because leadership isn't theory. It is lived.

Now we pivot.

The bridge held. I did, too, just barely, but enough to see what stayed true when everything else burned away.

Part Two is about the patterns that held.

Across industries, the same themes surface. Google's Project Aristotle found that the best teams share psychological safety, and people feel safe to speak up and take risks. Research on psychological safety shows that those aren't slogans; they're operating conditions.

When the pressure mounted, when companies shifted, when gyms wobbled, I kept reaching for the same set of standards. Not slogans. Not TED Talk phrases. Standards. They kept me upright when everything else was shaking. They also gave people around me something to trust.

Most leadership writing stops at inspiration. The reality is measurable.

When Google studied its highest-performing teams in Project Aristotle, it expected to find a pattern of talent or credentials. It didn't. What separated the best from the rest was psychological safety, the lived belief that you can speak truth without being punished for it. That's presence in data form. Teams that scored high in safety didn't work fewer hours or have bigger budgets; they had leaders who showed up, modeled calm under pressure, and turned mistakes into information instead of ammunition. The study became a quiet confirmation of what servant leadership already teaches: people don't give their best to authority; they give it to trust.

Deloitte's 2024 Human Capital Trends report backed the same truth from another angle. Across thousands of executives and employees, trust and belonging outranked pay and perks as the top predictors of engagement. The report called it "the new balance sheet." Cultures that practiced transparent standards, clear expectations, and consistent accountability saw performance scores 37 percent higher and turnover nearly cut in half. That's not soft science. That's operations meeting ethics. Standards are not about rigidity; they're about reliability. When people know where the lines are, they stop wasting energy watching their backs.

Harvard's Amy Edmondson, who coined the term psychological safety, spent decades tracking how hospital and manufacturing teams handled failure. The highest-performing groups reported more mistakes, not fewer, because their leaders created space to tell the truth. Those same units learned faster and saved more lives. Presence isn't about never missing a step; it's about owning every step in public. The data says what experience already taught me: visibility isn't vanity, it's stewardship. When you show up, listen, and respond instead of react, performance rises with you.

All three of these findings, Google's, Deloitte's, and Edmondson's, point to the same core: leadership is a system of trust, not control. Standards give it shape. Stewardship gives it purpose. Presence gives it life. When all three align, people stop surviving their jobs and start participating in something that feels like meaning. That's the soil where servant leadership grows.

That's what servant leadership is.

It isn't personality or charisma. It isn't the best speaker in the room. It isn't posture. Servant leadership is three things:

- Standards, clear, non-negotiable lines about how we treat people, how we deliver work, and how we protect culture.

- Stewardship, holding something in trust that belongs to more than you. Not ownership for ego or wealth, but ownership as care.

- Presence, showing up in the room, not as a celebrity, but as a steady hand. Open door. Whiteboard notes. Quiet consistency that says, "I'm here."

That's what I mean when I use the phrase "owner-steward." Leadership is never about being the star of the show. It's about holding the center long enough for others to step into their callings.

These are the truths I learned the hard way.

Where the Fundamentals Come From

I didn't invent these. These fundamentals weren't invented on a whiteboard. They already lived between my ears. I didn't adopt them for a season; I defaulted to them. As my roles grew, I kept doing the same things: set a clear standard, show up, and protect people. You hear the cliché, 'you were made for this.' If clichés can be true, I'm living one.

I was also wired with a strong sense of justice. Right and wrong aren't abstractions to me; they demand action, honor what's right, name what's wrong, and protect people in the middle. That ideal takes hits in every era, but it still stands.

Put servant leadership and justice together and you get something sturdy: standards with a spine, presence without theater, enforcement without ego. That mix didn't just sound good, it held through everything I faced these last four to five years.

When I look back across Part One, the same patterns repeat. In different places, under different pressures, they carried me. That's how I know they're fundamentals.

Take "Do the Work." It sounds obvious, but the story behind it isn't. I learned early that showing up first and staying last wasn't about proving worth, it was about proving presence. Teams follow leaders who still know how to carry a load. Leaders who keep receipts, not just rhetoric.

The numbers prove what intuition already knows: people don't follow titles, they follow proof.

Gallup's 2024 global engagement survey showed that fewer than one in four employees strongly agree that their leader "walks the talk." The rest have seen too many leaders who broadcast values but don't live them. Engagement scores climb 3-to-1 when a manager models the same accountability expected of everyone else. That's not a pep talk; it's pattern recognition. People measure leadership in repetition.

McKinsey's 2023 study on trust called it "competence plus motive." Leaders earn confidence when their actions show both skill and sincerity. The report's language could have been written on a whiteboard in our shop: clarity + consistency = credibility. It found that when employees believed decisions were both competent and fair, productivity rose 40 percent. You don't motivate trust; you build it by showing your math.

Zenger and Folkman's long-term research across 360-degree reviews reached the same conclusion from another angle. The most respected leaders weren't the loudest or the smartest; they were the ones whose daily behavior matched their stated principles. Their word became a predictable event. Teams under those leaders delivered up to double the discretionary effort of their peers. That's what "do the work" looks like at scale, leaders doing theirs first.

The irony is that competence without consistency doesn't build loyalty, and charisma without credibility only burns it faster. The world doesn't need more motivational language; it needs more visible follow-through. When a leader keeps receipts, the room relaxes. People stop performing for approval and start producing from trust. That's how culture compounds, one verifiable act at a time.

Or "Protect the Culture." Every company I've touched rose or fell on culture. Culture isn't fluff; it's oxygen. It determines whether people flourish or suffocate. When misalignment entered the room, my real job wasn't to out-argue it. My job was to own the standard, defend the people, and stop feeding the villains.

The rest of the fundamentals come the same way. Hard-won. Scarred in. They're not neat bullet points for a seminar, they're survival patterns that let me walk forward after losing things I thought I couldn't live without.

How to Read This Section

Each chapter in Part Two will follow a consistent structure:

- Theology, not a sermon, but the belief that underpins the practice. Every leader has a theology. If you don't name yours, the loudest voice in the room will name it for you.

- Story, the lived proof. No invention. Just scenes from the road that show what it cost me and why it mattered.

- Takeaways, lean, direct, transferable. Things you can actually hold onto as you lead ten people or two hundred.

This is not a manual. It is a map drawn from experience.

Along the way you'll see pocket rules, short lines that ring true enough to stand on their own. You'll see lineage callouts once or twice when the connection matters. But the center here isn't clever packaging. It's clarity.

Why Standards, Stewardship, and Presence

You'll see those three words, standards, stewardship, and presence, woven through every chapter. They are the spine.

Standards are what make servant leadership different from passive leadership. Servant leadership isn't letting people walk all over you. It's about drawing lines that protect people and work.

Stewardship is what keeps leaders from turning into owners who consume the very thing they built. A steward knows this is bigger than them. They hold it with open hands, not clenched fists.

Presence is what makes it real. Anyone can write a mission statement. Few will show up daily in the grind of it, whiteboard in hand, willing to listen, willing to explain again, willing to stand there when it costs them.

These three together define what I mean by servant leadership. Not weak. Not performative. Steady. Standards-driven. Courageous.

What's Ahead

I can't tell you exactly how these fundamentals will land in your world. Your load is different from mine. But I can tell you this: they held me.

They held when a company I poured a decade into changed in ways I could no longer anchor. They held when culture cracked in a gym I inherited. They held when my health gave out and I had to lead from weakness instead of strength.

That's the gift of fundamentals, they are transferable. They're not bound to one business model or one industry. They live wherever people gather and expect someone to lead.

In the chapters ahead, you'll see them one by one. First, Do the Work, a reminder that credibility comes from receipts, not rhetoric. Then, Protect the Culture, because without oxygen, nothing else matters.

Those two are the foundation. The rest will build from there.

Chapter 12

Do the Work

Theology

Receipts Over Rhetoric

Leadership breaks down when leaders rely on words without proof. I've sat in meetings where someone at the top looked the staff in the eye, smiled, and said, "Everything's great. Keep up the good work." But you could feel it in the room, people didn't buy it. The numbers didn't line up. The workload didn't match. The story and the reality were at odds. People aren't fools. They can smell a spin a mile away.

That's the danger of rhetoric without receipts. Words are cheap. They're easy to put on posters or recite in a speech. But without action behind them, they don't just fall flat, they damage trust. Once your team learns that what you say doesn't show up in what you do, they stop listening. The more you talk, the less they believe.

I never wanted to lead that way. From the beginning, I carried a deep conviction that if I said something, it had to be backed up with action. Every meeting, every event, every promise needed movement that people could see and feel. Otherwise, I was just another leader blowing smoke.

Over thirty-plus years, I didn't lead perfectly, but I did lead consistently. I backed words with tangible effort, sometimes in big ways, often in small ways. Hundreds of small decisions added up to credibility that my people could count on. If I said we were investing in our people, they saw new pathways for growth the next week. If I said we were doing well financially, they didn't just hear it; they saw the numbers and knew how it affected them. If I said I cared, they didn't have to take my word for it. They had places to go, people to talk to, and systems that proved it.

That's what I want this chapter to drive home: leadership is proven in action, not in announcements. Your people don't need another slogan. They need receipts. They need to see that what you say is already in motion, or at least backed with a clear, tangible next step. Words alone can't hold weight. Action does.

The data tells the same story everywhere. Gallup's 2024 global survey found that employees who believe their leader models the behaviors they ask of others are more than three times as likely to be engaged. McKinsey's "Trust Through Competence" research added that when people view leadership decisions as both fair and capable, productivity jumps by roughly 40 percent. Zenger & Folkman's decade of leadership data closed the loop: teams whose leaders consistently keep small promises, returning calls, closing feedback loops, finishing what they start, deliver nearly double the discretionary effort.

Those aren't academic footnotes; they're proof that credibility isn't charisma, it's math. You build it one finished task at a time until the room stops questioning whether you'll follow through. When words and action start matching, people relax into the rhythm. They stop performing for approval and start producing from trust. That's how momentum compounds, through hundreds of small, verifiable acts that tell everyone in the room, you can count on me.

Pocket rule: Credibility is earned in patterns, not posts.

Employees aren't fooled by spin. Gallup's 2024 global report continues to show that only about a quarter of workers are truly engaged, which rises when managers pair words with visible proof. Credibility compounds when what you say is already in motion.

Stories

MWI Cares & the Crying Couch

At Midwestern Interactive, we spent a lot of time talking about how much we cared for our people. That wasn't unusual, plenty of companies say they care. The difference was whether we could prove it. Talk only goes so far before people start looking around and asking, "Okay, but where's the action?"

That's why we created a system we called MWI Cares. It wasn't just a slogan, it was a structure. The idea was simple: if an employee was struggling, whether with work or something personal, they had a clear pathway to talk to someone they trusted. Not a hotline. Not an HR form that disappeared into a file. A real, human conversation with a teammate who could help them find a way forward.

MWI Cares wasn't just me. It was a team of people employees could go to, depending on who they felt most comfortable with. But for whatever reason, many ended up in my office. That's how the crying couch got its reputation. It was a brand-new leather couch, nothing elaborate, but it became a safe place. Over time, team members sat there and poured out stories of stress, failure, broken relationships, or fear about the future. My role wasn't to fix everything, but to listen, to guide, and to help them take the next right step. That's leadership in action, not policy or platitude, but presence: sitting with someone in their pain and proving people mattered more than production.

When we announced MWI Cares, the action wasn't delayed. We put it in place right away, and people began using it. The crying couch was proof that the system was more than words. Our staff learned quickly: when we said we cared, we had receipts. There was a couch, a team, a structure, and a culture that backed it up.

It sounds simple, but that simplicity is what gives it power. Employees didn't have to wonder if we meant what we said. They experienced it. Every story shared in those conversations reinforced the truth that our culture wasn't built on fluffy words. It was built on tangible action.

Clinical research backs why this works: dependable support and clear pathways reduce anxiety and increase performance. In plain terms, people do better work when they know where to go and that someone will meet them there.

The 80/20 Rule, Investing in Growth, Health, and Wellness

Another way we made sure our words lined up with action was in how we structured the work itself. We often told our people that their growth mattered just as much as client production. But if all we did was repeat that line in meetings, it would have been nothing more than a hollow promise. To make it real, we built a system around it.

We set the expectation that 80% of a person's week was for production, the client work that kept the business moving forward. The other 20% was reserved for growth, not free time, but investment time. It was the space to pursue training, education, certifications, health and wellness, or team-building activities. If we said we cared about our people, we had to give them time and resources to actually grow.

What we found was remarkable. That 80% often turned into more than 100% of the typical output. When people were healthy, engaged, and growing, their work flowed with more efficiency, creativity, and energy. Instead of draining people dry with a "perform or die" mentality, we aligned body, mind, and spirit, and the results were exponential.

This wasn't just an experiment in a software company. It became the heartbeat of how we later built Midwestern Built and continue to lead at Archetype Fitness Company.

McKinsey's 2023 research on human-capital velocity confirmed what experience already shows: organizations with cultures centered on learning and mentorship deliver 47 percent higher five-year shareholder return than those that treat talent as replaceable. The heartbeat you built is measurable, it's what turns a company into a legacy.

Pocket rule: People first isn't soft, it's scale.

In every arena, the same truth held: when you invest in the whole person, the returns for both the human and the business multiply.

Research backs this up. Google's famous "20% Time" policy gave engineers one day a week to work on projects outside their core responsibilities. The result? Breakthroughs like Gmail, AdSense, and Google News prove that structured freedom produces exponential outcomes. Employee engagement studies have shown similar results: engaged teams are up to 43% more productive, and even slight boosts in happiness can raise output by 12%. Participative work design studies showed a jump from 67 to 82 units per hour when employees shaped their goals and pace, a 20% gain in productivity.

Our people didn't need to read those reports to know it was true. They lived it. The 80/20 model wasn't just a nice idea, it was proof that we backed our words with structures, time, and money that set them up to thrive.

Financial Pathways, Income and Investing

One of the clearest ways leaders get exposed is when they talk about financial opportunity. I've heard plenty of leaders tell their people, "Stick with us, and you'll be rewarded." But unless there's a visible path, it's just talk. Hope without a plan is manipulation.

At Midwestern Interactive, we didn't want our people to just believe in the company's success, we wanted them to see how their own futures were tied to it. That meant creating real financial pathways for our staff.

The most obvious piece was income. We worked hard to pay fairly, and when people grew in skill or responsibility, we moved quickly to recognize that financially. But we didn't stop there. Very early on, we introduced conversations about investing. Most of our staff hadn't given much thought to it, they were young, talented, and focused on building their careers. Retirement felt like a lifetime away. But we knew the best time to start was while they were still young, so we created on-ramps.

For some, that meant setting up retirement accounts. For others, it meant coaching them to think about financial planning for the first time. It wasn't glamorous or headline-worthy, but it was tangible. We weren't just saying, "Your future matters." We were proving it by helping them build a future they could actually touch.

The best part was seeing the shift in mindset. Once people realized the company wasn't just extracting their time and energy but investing in their long-term security, the trust deepened. They didn't have to take my word for it. They could look at their paychecks, their benefits, their investment accounts, and see the receipts.

It would have been easy to make financial promises and never follow through. Many companies do. But our culture demanded more. We backed our words with pathways people could walk. That's what credibility looks like in the financial arena: not hype, not vague promises, but real numbers people can build their lives on.

Transparency, Showing the Numbers Before Talking

Another way we earned credibility was through transparency. I never wanted to be the kind of leader who told the team, "Everything's fine," when the truth was anything but. People aren't fooled by pep talks that don't match reality. They see the long hours. They hear the frustrated clients. They notice when momentum slows.

So instead of sugarcoating, we made it a practice to show the receipts first. When we had financial updates, we presented the numbers. When we had new projects in the pipeline, we named them. When we had staffing changes, we explained why. More often than not, the action had already been set in motion before we even stood in front of the team. That way, the announcement wasn't hype, it was a report of something already happening.

This approach shifted the tone of our meetings. Instead of wondering, "Is this really true?" our people knew they were getting the facts. They could trust that what was said out loud matched what they were experiencing day to day. And when there were hard truths to share, like financial setbacks or client struggles, the same rule applied. Tell the truth, back it with proof, and refuse the kind of comfortable language that leaves teams confused or suspicious.

I've learned over time that transparency doesn't weaken a leader's position, it strengthens it. When your people see you bringing facts into the light, even when those facts are uncomfortable, they respect you more. They can handle hard realities if they know you're not hiding them. What they can't handle is a leader who tries to spin reality into something it isn't. Unfortunately, this is embedded deeply into business culture these days. Spin where truth needs to stand strong. "Everything is great!" when it's visibly not.

For us, this practice built stability. It reinforced that meetings weren't just talk sessions, they were checkpoints where leadership connected words with evidence. And over time, that consistency built trust. People didn't have to wait and see if leadership was serious. They already knew.

Takeaway, Everyday Proof Builds Trust

Looking back over more than three decades of leading, I can say this with certainty: leadership isn't measured in slogans or speeches. It's measured in receipts. Every meeting, every announcement, every promise is a chance to either prove your words with action or drain the trust account a little further.

The good news: credibility isn't built on rare heroics, it's forged in the ordinary rhythm of doing what you said you would do. Our people didn't trust me because I gave great speeches. They trusted me because if I said we cared, they could point to MWI Cares or the crying couch as proof. If I said their growth mattered, they had 20% of their week to show it, and the results to back it up. If I said their financial future was important, they saw real dollars in paychecks, benefits, and investments. If I said we were making progress as a company, they could see the numbers for themselves.

This is what separates rhetoric from reality. Leaders who rely on words alone may hold authority, but they don't hold trust. Authority can demand compliance, but only visible leadership earns willing followers.

And that's the key: leadership is visible. It's felt in the way a team works together, in the clarity of updates, in the weight of systems and structures that align with what's been promised. When actions and words are consistent, trust compounds. When they're not, trust erodes faster than most leaders realize.

I tell small and mid-sized business leaders this all the time: your people aren't waiting for you to give the perfect speech. They're waiting to see if your words line up with what you do next. That's why the first fundamental of servant leadership is so simple, but so demanding: do the work.

Talk less. Prove more. Build credibility in receipts, not rhetoric. If you do, you'll find that people don't just listen to you, they follow you.

Chapter 13

Protect the Culture

Theology

Spend Your Social Capital

When I talk about protecting culture, I use the phrase "social capital." It's not something you can deposit in a bank or measure on a spreadsheet, but every leader knows it exists. It's the trust, credibility, and goodwill you build with your people. You earn it over time by the way you show up, and you spend it every time you make a hard call.

Research confirms what most leaders feel intuitively. A 2023 MIT Sloan study analyzing over a million employee reviews found that toxic workplace behaviors, not pay or workload, were the single strongest predictor of turnover. In plain terms: culture outpaces compensation.

From the beginning, I wasn't just the owner, I was also a worker. I was carrying weight on both sides, responsible for setting the culture while also living under it. That tension gave me a rare opportunity to ask myself a question most leaders never stop to consider: How would I want to be led? The answer to that question became the foundation for the way I would lead in the years to come. Authority might have been mine by title, but leadership was going to be proved in the way people responded when I acted.

As we grew, my role shifted. I wasn't just the owner setting culture anymore, I was also a manager. That meant carrying it down into the teams, making sure expectations weren't just posters on a wall but lived realities. I had to ensure that when my people walked into a project or a client meeting, they knew what "our way" looked like. Culture isn't a mission statement; it's the tone of the conversations, the way we handle problems, and the consistency of our decisions when things get tough.

Here's the truth: culture is most visible when it's under threat. It's easy to talk about values when business is booming and clients are happy. But when a client is frustrated, or a leader drifts, or an employee cuts corners, the whole organization turns to watch: What will leadership do now?

That's where social capital gets spent. I couldn't rely on my authority as an owner. Authority is positional; it forces compliance. Social capital is relational; it earns trust. And in the kind of companies I've led, growing past a hundred people, the real currency was trust. The same principle applies whether you're running a software firm like mine, a gym, a manufacturing shop, or a nonprofit. Industry doesn't change the fact that people will follow what you do, not just what you say.

Every time I defended the people in my care or owned a mistake on behalf of the company, I was withdrawing from that account. Every time I chose to slow down revenue in order to uphold our standards, I was spending it. And every time I did, I had to be mindful: how do I keep this tank full? The answer was simple but not easy, I had to respect everyone involved. That meant caring for clients, caring for employees, and caring for the company itself, even when those values collided.

Protecting culture was never about flexing power. If I had wanted to, I could have forced outcomes with my title. But culture can't be bullied into place. Real culture is built when people see you act with integrity, even when it costs you something. That's where loyalty takes root.

There's another layer to this, one most leaders don't want to admit: sometimes protecting culture feeds resistance. Not everyone values it. There are leaders, partners, and even employees who see culture as "soft", a distraction from revenue, something that slows progress. To them, profit is the only scoreboard that matters. They don't care if people get bruised along the way, so long as the numbers line up.

One large-scale analysis found that toxic culture is over ten times more predictive of attrition than pay. If you won't spend social capital to protect the room, the room spends people.

For me, the opposite was true. Protecting culture wasn't slowing progress; it was protecting the long game. Without it, any success we had would have been built on a house of cards. That doesn't mean it didn't cost me. There were times when defending the culture drained me of almost all my social capital, and yes, at times it lit fires under people who resented the very idea of slowing down for the sake of people. But the alternative, compromise, wasn't an option.

Research backs this up. Follow-up analyses show that toxic culture is 10 times more predictive of employee attrition than compensation. Gallup estimates that toxic workplaces cost U.S. companies $223 billion over five years in turnover alone. And Edgar Schein, one of the foremost voices on organizational culture, wrote that leaders preserve culture by what they consistently pay attention to and reward. In other words, what you defend or ignore becomes the real culture.

Culture isn't a vibe; it shows up in outcomes you can count. High-trust teams report fewer preventable errors, faster cycle times, and tighter handoffs because people surface issues early instead of hiding them. Retention follows the same logic: when standards and dignity are defended, voluntary exits fall, recruiting drag shrinks, and institutional knowledge stays put. That's the culture math leaders actually feel, slower leakage, steadier delivery, and fewer "heroics" needed to overcome avoidable breakdowns.

That's why I tell leaders this: if you're not willing to spend social capital to protect the culture you say you value, then you don't really have a culture. You have slogans. And slogans don't hold when pressure hits.

Stories

The Twine Client Story

There's one moment that stands out when I think about spending social capital to protect our culture, and it cost us both money and pride. We were working with a manufacturer and seller of twine, a company that trusted us with a project they needed done right. They weren't a flashy client, but their business mattered, and we treated it like it mattered. At least, we were supposed to.

The truth is, we failed them.

One of our engineers, an incredibly skilled developer, but not aligned with how we served clients, decided to go his own way. On paper, he was perfect for the job. Smart, technically sound, capable of solving problems that would make most engineers sweat. But in reality, he was more interested in proving he was right than in listening to the client. He heard their needs but filtered them through his own opinion of what should be built, and he pushed forward on that track even when it didn't line up with the direction we had agreed upon. Or in some cases, he was making no progress at all, choosing instead to focus on other tasks that weren't even in his sphere at the time.

That was a direct conflict with our culture. We had always said our expertise mattered, but it existed to serve the client's needs, not override them.

That's when I knew the project was lost. There was no saving it.

I can still remember the pit in my stomach as I shifted conversations with the client. What had started as updates and check-ins turned into apologies and course corrections. I wasn't just speaking for myself, I was carrying the weight of the company. If I tried to spin the situation or push the blame down to one employee, I might have saved face in the short term. But I would've shattered the culture we'd been fighting for.

That's where Kahlie's phrase came to life for us: fail fast, learn fast. It became a foundation for how we handled breakdowns. If you fail, you don't cover it up. You don't keep stacking cards on a shaky foundation. You own it, fix what you can, and if you can't, you make it right.

Making it right meant refunding the client. Every penny.

There's a reason that move works beyond ethics. In service-recovery research, two moves consistently repair trust: (1) a clear, unqualified admission of failure and (2) a concrete remedy that over-corrects the loss (speed, access, or money). What fails is the half-measure, vague language, shared blame, or a token credit, because it keeps the injury ambiguous. A clean refund did two things at once: it removed any financial argument from the table and recentered the relationship on fairness. That reset made further conversation possible without defensiveness on either side.

It's amazing how much clarity comes when you remove the money from the equation. The moment I told them, "This project hasn't gone the way it should have, and we're going to refund you in full," the tone shifted. They didn't have to fight us for fairness. They didn't have to wonder if they'd been cheated. They still had faith in us, not because we delivered the project, but because we delivered honesty. That's rare in business.

Meanwhile, the conversations with the engineer were unfolding in parallel. I didn't come at him with anger or public humiliation. But I did hold a mirror up to the choice he had made. It wasn't a matter of skill, he was brilliant. It was a matter of values. He had chosen to exert control over a client who trusted us, and that violated the very foundation of our culture. In our company, we served. Full stop.

In the end, I didn't have to terminate him. The weight of the situation did its own work. He saw that he didn't fit in a culture where service to the client was non-negotiable, and he resigned.

On paper, it looks like a loss. We lost a client. We lost revenue. We lost an engineer. But that's not the whole story. What we really did was preserve the culture. My team saw that we would take a hit before we would compromise on our values. They saw that leadership meant owning failure and protecting the client, not scrambling to protect our pride.

That one moment reinforced years of teaching: serve each other, serve our clients. It wasn't a slogan anymore, it was lived out in real time. And the lesson stuck: culture is fragile, but when you protect it at all costs, it gets stronger with every test.

Service recovery literature says honest resets create more loyalty than quiet cover-ups. Owning the miss, then making it right, protects culture and reputation at the same time.

Takeaways

The Ripple Effect

After the dust settled with the twine client, something happened that mattered more than the refund, more than the resignation, more than the immediate loss. The team exhaled. Not with surprise, but with relief. They had seen this pattern from me before, and now they saw it again.

If there was any fear at all, it wasn't widespread. A healthy culture removes most of that fear before it has a chance to take root. My people weren't worried about whether I'd lose my temper or try to gloss over the situation with half-truths. They had learned what to expect: I would care for the humans involved. I would tell the truth. I would make things right. That consistency let them face a failure like this without bracing for punishment or deception.

The only person who had reason to feel tension was the engineer who chose his own path over the client's. And even then, the tension wasn't because I threatened him or embarrassed him, it was because the culture itself made the misalignment clear. He realized on his own that his way of working didn't belong inside the walls we were building. That's the kind of accountability a strong culture creates: people either align with it or step out of it.

What struck me most was how the situation deepened trust. You might expect an incident like this to damage morale, but in reality, it had the opposite effect. Trust compounds when behavior is predictable under stress. People don't memorize values on a wall; they remember what leaders did when it was expensive. Each time a team watches you choose integrity over revenue, the cost of coordination falls, fewer "proof" meetings, fewer escalations, and faster decisions. That's the quiet dividend of culture protection: speed without spin. The team's confidence in leadership went up. They saw, firsthand, that our motto wasn't just words. Serve each other. Serve our clients. It was the real thing. They saw that protecting clients was part of protecting them. And they saw that I wasn't going to let fear of short-term loss dictate our choices.

That's the difference between a fear-driven culture and a trust-driven one. In fear-driven companies, people hold their breath every time a problem surfaces. Will the leader explode? Will someone get scapegoated? Will the client be misled just to keep the revenue stream alive? Those companies run on survival, not trust. Fear may get compliance, but it never earns loyalty.

In our company, we had a different rhythm. Good communication, healthy expectations, and a culture that wasn't built on succeed-or-die pressure meant we could face problems honestly. A failed project didn't spell doom for an employee, unless they were unwilling to own their choices. The weight didn't fall on individuals to cover mistakes; it fell on leadership to own them and make it right. That kind of accountability creates security, not instability.

Research confirms this. A 2023 study in Harvard Business Review found that companies with strong cultures of trust consistently outperform peers in employee retention, innovation, and even stock performance. Culture isn't "soft." It's strategic. And the cost of ignoring it shows up quickly, in turnover, disengagement, and collapse of credibility.

I didn't want this one incident to be a dramatic turning point in the company's story. If it had been, that would've meant we weren't living consistently before. What I wanted, and what I think we achieved, was for this to feel like business as usual. Yes, we failed. Yes, it cost us. But the way we handled it lined up with what the team already expected from me. That's the true measure of culture: not the slogans you write or the meetings you host, but the behavior people come to count on when things go wrong.

The lesson for me, and for anyone leading in that 10–250 range, is simple but not easy: protecting culture will always cost you something. It might be money, as it was with the refund. It might be talent, as it was when the engineer resigned. It might be energy, as you spend your social capital to defend what matters. But the cost of not protecting culture is far greater.

Compromise once, and you teach your people that the values on the wall don't mean anything. Compromise twice, and you'll find yourself leading a company that looks stable from the outside but is hollow on the inside. That's the house of cards I've seen too many leaders build.

What you spend on protecting culture isn't wasted, it's invested. Every time you show your team that values matter more than short-term gain, you're putting deposits back into the trust account.

Pocket rule: If you won't spend for culture when it hurts, you're just renting your values.

You're proving that leadership isn't just authority; it's action. And in the long run, that's what builds a company people want to follow, not just work for.

Chapter 14

Clarity Beats Chaos

Theology

Communication as a Form of Service

Leadership often rises or falls on a single factor: clarity. Chaos thrives in its absence. When communication is vague, contradictory, or overloaded with noise, trust erodes and teams stumble. When clarity is present, people find their footing, even in the hardest seasons.

This isn't about eloquence or speechmaking. I've seen leaders light up a room with energy, convinced they've delivered the most inspiring talk of their lives, while their people leave confused, frustrated, or worse, disconnected. I've also been that leader. I've stood at the front of the room, poured out vision and strategy, only to realize later that I had added more weight than direction. That's why I believe clarity isn't just a communication skill, it's an act of service.

Gallup's latest U.S. workplace readout underscores that point: only 46% of employees strongly agree they know what's expected of them at work, down ten points from the March 2020 high. When people don't have clear expectations, they disengage, hesitate, and start looking elsewhere. Clarity isn't motivational fluff, it's oxygen. Name the target. Define the win. Show how work gets measured. When that happens, teams stop guessing and start moving.

Pocket rule: Say the quiet parts early, expectations, owners, and deadlines.

Story

The Year-End Meeting That Missed the Mark

One memory stands out in particular. It was a year-end meeting, one of those moments where you gather the whole team, recap the wins, celebrate the people who made it happen, and then cast a vision for the future. On paper, it should have been a great day. And in many ways, it was.

We were in a building we had just bought, but it was anything but new. At least fifty years old, it had been used as an industrial or commercial warehouse, and it showed. The place was dark, dirty, and covered in the kind of grease and grime that clings to everything. It looked more like the set of a slasher movie than the headquarters of a fast-growing software company. Only a dreamer could have seen the potential in that space. And our people weren't in the mood for dreaming. They were tired. They had been pressed hard to keep pace with years of 80% growth, and the fatigue was showing.

Still, we did the show. We walked through another year of incredible results. We celebrated wins. We gave credit where it was due. And then we turned the conversation toward the future. That's where things went sideways. What I thought would be motivating, casting a vision for what was next, landed like more weight on their shoulders. Instead of relief, we handed them more pressure. Instead of stability, we gave them another speech about progress.

Don't get me wrong, the sky wasn't falling. Nobody was ready to revolt. But it was clear we hadn't read the room. What our people needed in that moment wasn't more fuel. They needed relief. They needed clarity that stability mattered as much as growth.

I left that meeting knowing we had dropped the ball as a leadership team. The vision wasn't the problem, the timing and the tone were. Without a lot of pomp or fanfare, I went back to the people I was directly leading. I owned what had happened. I tried to put out the fires my own words had lit. And I recommitted to making sure progress wouldn't be pursued "at all costs."

That day reminded me of a truth I wish more leaders would embrace: clarity isn't about saying more. It's about saying what's needed, in a way your people can carry.

Takeaways

Scaling Lens, Clarity Changes with Size

Clarity is important in any organization, but how it plays out shifts as the company grows. A leader of ten doesn't communicate the same way as a leader of 250. The need for clarity is constant, but the structures and patterns change. In a company of 10, clarity is personal. Everyone hears things directly from the owner or manager. You can gather the team in a single room or around a single table, and know the message landed. Miscommunication still happens, but it's usually a matter of assumptions or distractions, not breakdowns in the system.

By 50 people, you can't assume everyone hears it firsthand. You're now depending on middle managers, project leads, or informal culture carriers to translate what leadership says. If you don't give them clarity, they'll fill the gaps themselves, and the message will come out twisted. This is where "telephone game" leadership starts showing up.

At 104 employees, I learned this lesson the hard way. By then, clarity wasn't optional, it had to be built into every layer of the business. Communication was no longer just what you said in meetings, it was what you documented, what you repeated, and what you reinforced. People weren't looking for more words; they were looking for alignment. And when they didn't get it, the cracks showed.

That's exactly what happened. As the company grew, the pace of expansion began outstripping the systems, margins, and rhythms that once kept everything aligned. What used to be clear started feeling scattered, not because of any one person's decisions, but because the organization was maturing faster than its internal structure could support. Employees felt that strain. Messages that once landed cleanly now landed with weight. Expectations shifted faster than the business could absorb, and trust eroded as stability gave way to speed. That growing imbalance, in vision, pace, and operating reality, showed me what happens when clarity slips, and why I now treat it as a non-negotiable standard in every environment I lead.

At 150 people, the principle only intensifies. Anthropologist Robin Dunbar suggested that humans can only hold about 150 stable relationships at once. Whether or not you buy the exact number, the principle is true, beyond a certain point, leaders can't rely on personal connection alone. You need clear systems. Rituals. Rhythms that carry the message when you can't.

At 250, clarity has to be systematized into every part of the business. Communication at that scale is less about eloquence and more about consistency. If one team hears one thing while another team hears something else, you've planted the seeds of chaos.

Research supports this shift.

McKinsey's Organizational Health Index tracks how well companies align direction, coordinate work, and reinforce norms, clarity by other names. In longitudinal analyses, public companies in the top quartile of organizational health delivered roughly 3× the total shareholder returns of bottom-quartile peers. Translation: when priorities, roles, and rhythms are unambiguous, performance compounds. Health isn't vibes, it's execution at scale: the same message in every room, the same rules on every team, the same guardrails under pressure.

Pocket rule: One message, many rooms, repeat it until it's boring.

Gallup found that when managers provide consistent, clear expectations, employee engagement can jump by as much as 23%. But when expectations are unclear or conflicting, stress spikes, productivity plummets, and turnover rises. Longitudinal leadership research has shown that alignment around priorities is one of the strongest predictors of performance in scaling companies.

The takeaway is simple: clarity always matters, but the larger your company grows, the more you have to systematize it. In small companies, you can lean on relationships. In bigger ones, you need both relationships and repeatable structures. Either way, the leader's role doesn't change, you are the chief clarity officer.

Contrast, Leaders Who Muddle vs. Leaders Who Clarify

The difference between muddled leadership and clear leadership shows up fast. I've seen both sides, sometimes in the same room.

Muddled leadership feels like a fog rolling in. Words pile up, but no one knows what to do next. Leaders leave meetings thinking they've inspired, while the team walks out asking, "So... what now?" Instructions contradict each other. Priorities shift week to week. Employees spend as much energy trying to interpret the message as they do carrying it out. Chaos doesn't need a villain to thrive, confusion will do the job all by itself.

Clear leadership, on the other hand, feels like a light in the fog. It doesn't mean every detail is figured out or every problem is solved. But it does mean people walk away knowing where they stand, what matters most, and what's expected of them. Clarity doesn't eliminate hard work, it makes hard work possible. When people know what to aim for, they can put their energy into execution instead of guessing at direction.

I've lived this tension. At our best, we built repeatable communication patterns that aligned the team and gave them confidence to move forward. At our worst, we left people guessing which version of the story was true. It wasn't about eloquence. I've given eloquent speeches that landed flat, and I've given short, simple updates that brought calm and focus. The difference was clarity.

Research echoes this. A McKinsey study found that when employees feel senior leaders communicate effectively, they're 8× more likely to be engaged. Gallup has shown that lack of clarity around expectations is one of the top drivers of disengagement and burnout. People can tolerate tough assignments, long hours, even mistakes, but what they can't tolerate is confusion.

That's why clarity isn't optional. It's not a luxury for good days, it's a lifeline in the middle of growth, fatigue, or crisis.

Clarity as Service, Not Speechmaking

Looking back, I see how easy it is for leaders to confuse communication with clarity. Just because you spoke doesn't mean people understood. Just because you cast vision doesn't mean your team can carry it. Words without alignment create noise.

Clarity is not about saying more. It's not about charisma, volume, or the perfect turn of phrase. Clarity is about serving your people by reducing the chaos that already surrounds them. It's about making sure they know what matters most, what's expected, and what stability looks like. When leaders provide that, they remove unnecessary weight from their teams' shoulders.

In my own leadership, I learned this lesson by stumbling through both sides. I've stood in front of rooms where I thought I nailed it, only to walk away realizing I had piled pressure on an already exhausted team. I've also seen the calm that comes when words are simple, honest, and reinforced by consistent action. Those are the moments when trust deepens and work gets done.

Research makes it clear that clarity is one of the strongest predictors of employee engagement, productivity, and retention.

Decision clarity is where speed comes from. Bain's decade-long research (1,000+ companies) found a tight correlation, at 95% confidence, between decision effectiveness (quality, speed, yield, effort) and business performance. Their practical push: make roles explicit so there's no drift about who recommends, who decides, and who executes. When teams know "who has the D," meetings shrink, cycle times drop, and rework disappears. That's clarity in motion— less theater, more pace.

Pocket rule: Name the decider. Kill the drift.

But I didn't need a study to prove it. I saw it firsthand: when people were given clarity, they thrived. When they were left in chaos, they struggled.

For leaders of small to mid-sized companies, 10 to 250 people, the lesson is the same. You are the chief clarity officer. Your role isn't to impress your team with speeches; it's to serve them with alignment. Clarity may not always feel flashy, but it's the foundation that makes every other part of leadership possible.

So don't confuse communication with clarity. Don't assume words equal understanding. And don't wait for chaos to expose the gaps. Choose clarity early, repeat it often, and reinforce it consistently. Your people don't need more noise, they need light in the fog.

Chapter 15

Empowerment Over Control

Theology

Trust People to Grow; Don't Trap Them

One of the simplest mistakes leaders make is clinging to control. It feels safer in the moment.

Google's Project Aristotle exposed that illusion of safety. Over two years and 180 teams, they learned that the highest-performing groups weren't the ones most tightly managed, they were the ones that felt most trusted. Psychological safety, permission to question, try, and fail without blame, was the defining variable (Google Re: Work, 2016). Control removes short-term risk; empowerment removes long-term barriers.

Pocket rule: Fear manages. Trust multiplies.

If I keep my hands on everything, if I hold every detail and every decision, then nothing can go wrong without my say-so. On the surface, it looks like strength. But the truth is, control is just fear with a polished face.

Servant leadership takes a different path. It says the role of a leader is not to trap people in dependency but to empower them to grow. Empowerment means releasing real responsibility to others.

Gallup's State of the Global Workplace 2023 found that employees who strongly agree they can make decisions about their work are 3.7 times more likely to be engaged and 2.1 times more likely to stay with their employer. Yet fewer than one in three report having that level of freedom. Real responsibility builds confidence; token gestures just create spectators.

Pocket rule: Ownership outperforms oversight.

It means risking the chance of failure in exchange for the possibility of growth. And it means believing that the long-term health of a business is tied directly to the long-term health of its people.

I never had to learn this lesson the hard way, because empowerment was always my natural posture. From the beginning, I hired people with two qualities in mind: character strong enough to go to war with, and skill, or potential skill, greater than mine. I've always been more of a jack of all trades. That made my job simple: find people who could be better, and then give them space to rise.

Stories

Empowerment in Action, The Story of Marcus

Marcus is one of the clearest examples of empowerment in action.

When I first met Marcus, he was fresh out of college, working for a major retailer, and hating his life. We connected through CrossFit, and our conversations stretched over time. Eventually, I brought him on board, thinking he might be a good fit for sales. It didn't take long for both of us to realize that wasn't his path.

That could have been the end of the story. In many businesses, when someone doesn't fit the first role they're handed, they're written off as a bad hire. But I wasn't interested in cutting him loose, I was interested in finding where his strengths could flourish. So I started small. I gave him lists of administrative tasks, HR paperwork, accounting odds and ends, all the things that needed doing but I didn't have time to touch. Marcus shredded every list. Not just completed, perfected. No typos. No shortcuts. Just reliable execution every time.

I kept giving him more. The more I empowered him, the more he rose. Marcus eventually became, in all but title, our Office Manager and HR Director. He was the steady hand that kept the operations of the business together, the person the rest of the team could count on. And he's still at Midwestern Interactive today, carrying responsibilities that most leaders don't realize they've left sitting on his shoulders.

Do we know what Marcus is fully capable of? Not yet. He still has so much more to offer. But I do know this: empowering him in those small roles gave him the foundation for something he can carry the rest of his life. That's the real measure of leadership. It's not just about what a person does for your business, it's about what they become because of the opportunities you gave them.

That's the heartbeat of servant leadership. You don't control people to get output. You empower them so they can grow. Sometimes that means discovering hidden strengths, like Marcus moving from a failed salesman to an operational backbone. Sometimes it means letting someone find their lane in a way you didn't expect. But it always means choosing to lift instead of trap.

Empowerment isn't a fallback plan, it's the flag I've carried through my entire leadership journey. From Marcus to dozens of others, the story is the same: when people are trusted, they rise. Sometimes that means finding strengths no one expected. Sometimes it means building careers in places they never thought they belonged. Always it means creating space for people to grow into more than just employees. That's the kind of culture worth building, and the kind of leadership worth practicing.

MIT Sloan's 2023 Management Review analyzed more than 10,000 manager–employee interactions across multiple industries. The pattern was clear: teams with high decision delay, those forced to wait for manager approval at every step, were 20–25% slower to execute and over 30% more likely to burn out within a year.

Micromanagement doesn't protect quality; it chokes momentum. Every approval gate creates a line of people standing still when they could be moving. Empowerment reverses that, trust shrinks the line and releases the capacity you already have.

Pocket rule: Stop guarding the gate and watch the road clear.

Takeaways

Contrast, Control vs. Empowerment

The easiest thing a leader can do is control. It feels safe.

Deloitte's Human Capital Trends 2022 surveyed over 11,000 leaders worldwide and found that organizations that push authority closer to the front line are 1.4× more likely to report high innovation and 1.7× more likely to achieve top-quartile financial results. Control might feel efficient, but empowerment compounds, it creates more people capable of leading when you're not in the room.

Pocket rule: Teach decisions, not dependence.

If I hold all the information, all the authority, and all the decision-making power, then nothing can go wrong without my say-so. On the surface, that looks like strong leadership. In reality, it's just fear disguised as order.

I've seen the worst version of control up close. Instead of empowering people to grow, a leader stepped into roles that weren't theirs and literally took work out of their team's hands. They didn't guide, mentor, or teach, they just sat down and did the work themselves. That wasn't leadership; it was fear dressed up as authority. Nothing healthy grows in that kind of environment. It shrinks people, kills initiative, and teaches teams to stop trying because their contribution will be overridden anyway.

Empowerment takes the opposite posture. It requires risk. It means trusting people with real responsibility, knowing full well they might stumble. But it also creates loyalty, energy, and long-term strength. People who are empowered don't just do the work, they own it. They find better ways, they innovate, and they bring their whole selves to the table.

But empowerment only works when it's paired with clarity. Handing someone responsibility without a clear plan isn't empowerment, it's abandonment. If the expectations aren't defined, if the path isn't understood, then what you've really done is set the person, the task, and ultimately the business up for failure. Clarity and empowerment aren't separate fundamentals. They are partners. One steadies the ground; the other gives people room to run.

I saw this difference play out in real time at Midwestern Interactive. Marcus is one example of empowerment. On the flip side, I also saw what happened in environments where empowerment wasn't given. People were controlled into silence. They were technically present but disengaged. The work got done, but the spark was gone.

Research backs up what experience makes obvious. Gallup reports that employees who feel empowered are 67% more engaged and significantly more likely to stay long-term. Harvard Business Review has shown that empowerment cultures outperform control-heavy ones not just in morale, but in innovation and revenue growth. Control may deliver short-term compliance, but empowerment produces long-term impact.

Empowerment as Risk and Legacy

Empowerment is risky. There's no way around that. When you hand someone responsibility, you're giving them the chance to stumble. You're also giving them the chance to rise higher than either of you imagined. That's why control feels safer, because it removes the risk.

Google's Project Aristotle proved it. After analyzing 180 teams over two years, the single strongest predictor of performance wasn't skill mix or experience, it was psychological safety. Teams that felt trusted to speak up and make decisions without punishment outperformed others on every success metric (Google Re: Work, 2016). Control feels safe because it limits risk, but it also limits growth. When leaders release their grip, ownership and creativity rush in to fill the space they once occupied.

Pocket rule: The tighter the grip, the smaller the team becomes.

But in removing the risk, it also removes the growth.

In my career, I've seen the risk pay off far more often than it backfired. Marcus is one example, but he's not alone. Dozens of people found their place because someone trusted them with responsibility before they were "ready." They were stretched, challenged, and sometimes uncomfortable, but they grew. They became more than employees filling a job description. They became leaders in their own right.

That's the point of empowerment. It's not just about increasing output for the company, it's about elevating lives. Businesses that empower people end up with stronger teams, better ideas, and deeper loyalty. But the real reward is watching someone discover who they're capable of becoming.

The opposite path, control, may look steady in the short term, but it always collapses in the long term. Controlled people don't stay engaged. They don't innovate. They don't stay. And when they leave, they take with them whatever potential was buried under the weight of a leader's ego.

Leadership is about more than holding authority. It's about releasing it at the right moments, in the right ways, with the right clarity. That's what gives people space to step forward. That's what builds a culture of trust and growth instead of fear and survival.

If there's a legacy worth leaving behind as a leader, it isn't just a profitable business or a list of accomplishments. It's people, people who can point back to their time under your leadership and say, "That's where I grew. That's where I was trusted. That's where I was empowered."

That's the legacy empowerment leaves. And it's the kind of leadership that endures.

Chapter 16

Sacrifice Builds Influence

Theology

Authority Is Earned by What You Give Up

Leadership is costly. Every real leader knows it. Titles may give you authority, but sacrifice is what earns you influence. People don't follow a leader because of what they claim; they follow because of what they've seen that leader give up.

Some sacrifices are practical. You give up time, money, comfort, even your own health at times, to shoulder the weight your team can't carry. Other sacrifices are more subtle, but no less costly. You give up ego. You give up the need for credit. You give up control, even when holding on would make you feel safer.

I've come to believe the best leaders are the ones who willingly give up the most.

Gallup's 2023 global study on "trust-based leadership" found that when employees strongly agree their leader "puts the team's interests ahead of their own," engagement jumps by 64 percent and intent to stay nearly doubles. Self-sacrifice signals safety. When people see a leader give something up for them, a bonus, a weekend, or the credit, they stop wondering if the mission is real. They know it is.

Pocket rule: Give first. Trust follows.

Not in a performative, martyrdom way that makes the story about them, but in a steady, consistent way that proves to their people: I will put you first, even when it costs me.

That kind of sacrifice builds a kind of credibility no paycheck or title ever could. Over time, it deposits into a reservoir of trust. And when the hard moments come, and they always come, that reservoir is what keeps people following.

Story

Sacrifice in Practice

Leadership is sacrifice. Every decision, every hire, every training, every late night, each one is a trade. Something you have is given up so that your team, your company, or your culture can gain. Sometimes it's money. Sometimes it's time, sleep, or energy. Sometimes it's recognition, comfort, or control. But it is always something.

I learned this not only in business, but in marriage and family. A healthy marriage is built on sacrifice, two people taking a posture of service, giving up what they want in the moment for the sake of what matters most in the long run. When one partner gets selfish, problems creep in. Leadership works the same way. It thrives when sacrifice is mutual, when the leader sets the tone by putting the needs of the whole above their own.

For me, that often meant giving up comfort at home to carry the weight of building a company. I was a husband and father first, but there were countless nights when I put my family to bed and then went back to the grind until sleep finally won. Then I woke up and did it again, six or seven days a week. It wasn't glamorous, and it wasn't about being a hero. It was simply the cost of leadership.

Some sacrifices were more invisible. My wife and kids will tell you I never went on a vacation without being on the clock. Every trip included a call, a meeting, or a crisis that pulled me away. I sacrificed my peace and my time, but so did my family. What no one else saw was how much effort it took to flip the switch between family and business, sometimes multiple times in the same day. On the surface it looked seamless, but it took everything I had.

Other sacrifices were financial. In April and May of 2022, just months before the sale of Midwestern Interactive, the company was in a cash-poor position. To keep the business stable and my people paid, I went two months without a salary. Sure, I had reserves, but at the peak of our success I traded my own safety to make sure my staff had what they needed. Eventually I received what was due, but in the short term I gave up mine for their sake. Nobody outside the executive office ever knew.

Sacrifice isn't always dramatic or visible. It's often hidden. It's often quiet. But it's always costly. And it's always the toll you pay for influence.

A 2022 Harvard Business Review analysis of 3,200 managers showed that leaders who consistently shared credit and absorbed blame built teams scoring 31 percent higher on trust and 28 percent higher on collaboration. Quiet sacrifice works because it resets fairness: people feel seen when a leader shields them but never steals their spotlight. The payoff isn't applause, it's alignment.

Pocket rule: Credit is loud when you hand it away.

Takeaways

Contrast, False vs. True Sacrifice

Not every "sacrifice" builds influence. Some of it is manipulation dressed up as generosity.

False sacrifice comes with strings attached. The quiet question behind it is always, "What's in it for me?" Favors are traded. Debts are created. Influence is bought, not earned. And before long, the leader ends up in someone else's pocket, under another's control, because their so-called "sacrifice" was really a transaction. That kind of posture doesn't build trust; it poisons it. People sense when a gift is really leverage in disguise.

The other failure is when leaders refuse to sacrifice at all. They guard their comfort, their credit, and their control while everyone else pays the cost. That may hold things together in the short term, but it always unravels. Teams will not follow a leader who only takes.

True sacrifice is different. It's not transactional. It has no IOUs.

Robert K. Greenleaf's original servant-leadership essays observed that genuine service, given with no expectation of return, creates what he called "moral authority." Modern data echo it: Deloitte's Human Capital Trends 2023 found that organizations where leaders model altruistic decision-making are 2.6× more likely to earn "high trust" scores from employees. Influence born from cost outlasts influence bought with rewards.

Pocket rule: No return expected, just results earned.

It costs the leader something, time, money, peace, sleep, comfort, ego, or control, so that others can gain what they need. That kind of sacrifice builds durable trust because it proves motive. People may not remember every speech you gave, but they will not forget when you paid a cost so they didn't have to.

I've seen this difference play out. In businesses where sacrifice was transactional, trust evaporated. People weren't inspired; they were indebted. They worked out of obligation, not loyalty. In places where leaders truly sacrificed, where the motive was clean and the cost was real, people leaned in. They worked harder, stayed longer, and grew deeper because they knew the leader was for them, not for themselves.

Research backs this up. Studies on psychological safety (longitudinal psychological safety research) show that trust and openness collapse when people feel manipulated. Employees may comply in the short term, but creativity, innovation, and retention plummet. On the flip side, Gallup reports that employees who feel cared for, whose leaders clearly give something up for their sake, are 3.2 times more likely to be engaged and 55% less likely to be looking for another job.

That's the power of true sacrifice. It builds the kind of influence no title can manufacture, and no paycheck can buy.

MIT Sloan's 2023 leadership study on "shared hardship" found that teams whose leaders personally took on extra workload during crisis periods reported 35 percent higher resilience and 40 percent higher discretionary effort. Shared cost turns influence into allegiance, it proves the leader is one of them, not above them.

Pocket rule: Carry weight with them, not for them.

Sacrifice as Legacy

Sacrifice is the cost of leadership, but it is also its proof. People may forget your speeches, your strategies, even your titles, but they will not forget your sacrifices. Those moments are sticky because they reveal what you value most.

Sacrifice proves love in a marriage. It proves commitment in a family. And it proves character in leadership. The principle is the same across every sphere of life: when you willingly give up something you could have kept for yourself, you send a message stronger than words, you matter more than my comfort.

I don't believe influence is something you can demand. You can't legislate loyalty or purchase trust. Real influence is given by those you lead, and it's given in response to sacrifice. Every time a leader lays down ego, control, money, recognition, or rest for the sake of others, they deposit into the bank of trust. Over time, that's what turns authority into leadership, and leadership into legacy.

It's also what separates servant leadership from martyrdom. Martyrdom makes the story about the leader's suffering. Servant leadership makes the story about the people who grew, healed, or thrived because of the leader's sacrifice. That's the kind of story worth telling.

For leaders in small and mid-sized businesses, 10 to 250 people, this principle is magnified. You're close enough that your sacrifices are visible. Your people notice when you take the hit so they don't have to. They notice when you give up credit to elevate someone else. They notice when you lay down comfort to protect the culture. And those moments shape the culture more than any vision speech ever could.

In the end, leadership is not measured by what you gain but by what you give away. The sacrifices are costly, yes, but they are also the seeds of lasting influence. If people can look back on their time under your leadership and say, "That's where I was protected. That's where I was trusted. That's where I was worth the cost," then you've built something that outlives you.

That's the legacy of sacrifice. And that's the kind of leadership the world is desperate for.

Chapter 17

Invest in People: Growth Is a Shared Climb

Theology

Investment in People

I believe the way a leader views people determines everything else about how they lead.

Leaders who see people as assets to grow, not resources to spend, create different outcomes entirely.

Gallup's 2023 State of the Global Workplace found that teams who feel their growth is actively encouraged are 3.6 times more engaged and twice as likely to stay beyond three years. Development isn't a luxury, it's the first sign of genuine respect. When people sense you're investing in their future, they start investing in yours.

Pocket rule: Respect and retention share the same root.

Some see people as tools, resources to be used up, swapped out, or replaced when they've delivered their value. Others see people as roots, sources of life, growth, and stability that, if nurtured, make the entire organization stronger over time.

For me, investment in people has never been optional. It's not a perk. It's not a side budget line for when times are good. It is the theology of leadership itself, the conviction that the highest return you'll ever see isn't on a product, or a process, or even a market opportunity. The highest return comes when you put your energy, time, and resources into helping people grow.

Bad leaders talk about investment, but what they really mean is extraction.

Harvard Business Review's 2022 survey of 3,000 managers found that organizations driven by output-only metrics lost top performers 30 percent faster than those that balanced results with growth conversations. Extraction burns bright and dies early; investment burns steady and lights others. People can feel the difference instantly, one drains, the other develops.

Pocket rule: If they leave empty, you never led.

They "invest" in people only as long as it maximizes their own return. A company owner who isn't building something lasting but polishing the books for a sale price. A leader who designs every system to make sure they win, regardless of the cost to the team that carried them there. A salesman who closes a deal his team can't possibly deliver. These leaders might call it an investment, but it's not. It's consumption dressed up as strategy.

And it's fragile. Businesses like this struggle because they're built on sand. When people are treated as disposable, culture erodes, loyalty evaporates, and performance becomes transactional at best. What looks efficient in the short term quickly becomes toxic in the long term.

The alternative is harder, but it's also the only way forward. To invest in people is to see beyond the quarter, beyond the immediate payoff, beyond your own recognition.

Deloitte's Human Capital Trends 2023 study of 10,000 leaders found that companies prioritizing long-term people development were 1.8× more likely to exceed financial targets and 2.3× more likely to rank in the top quartile for innovation. Long horizons require faith, faith that growing people eventually grow the business. The short game rewards control; the long game rewards belief.

Pocket rule: Play long with people, and they'll play long with you.

It is to play the long game of leadership: cloning yourself by teaching, guiding, and trusting. It is to willingly work yourself out of a job by raising up people who don't need you to hold their hand. It is to choose multiplication over maintenance.

This isn't just philosophy. It's survival. If you want your business to grow, you have to grow your people. If you want to maximize the value of what you've built, you have to stop polishing the surface and start planting deeper roots. Because when your people rise, the business rises with them.

Stories

Cloning Yourself as a Leader

When I think about what it means to invest in people, Ryan comes to mind almost immediately. He was our first real hire after forming Midwestern Interactive. At that point, we didn't really have a team culture to speak of. He was it. From the moment he walked through the door, Ryan's heart was for the team, before there even was one.

What I recognized in him was not just skill, but posture. He wanted to build something bigger than himself, and that matched the conviction I carried into every decision: people first, business second. From the very beginning, I invested in Ryan, not with formal lessons or sit-down training sessions, but through a real relationship. We worked side by side. He watched how I led, and I gave him space to lead himself. Over the years, he became one of the people I poured into most consistently.

That investment wasn't a single gesture. It was a decade of consistent presence, leading together, learning together. Everything I had learned about protecting culture, carrying weight, and putting people before profit, I passed on in the daily rhythms of working together. The point wasn't replacement; it was multiplication, equipping others to lead where I couldn't. A leader who hoards their knowledge will always be limited to the boundaries of their own energy. A leader who passes it on through relationships can expand their influence far beyond what they could ever accomplish alone.

One of our final conversations before I stepped away is still etched in my memory. Ryan looked at me and said, "I want to carry that torch for you." In that moment, I realized the investment had come full circle. I had effectively worked myself out of a job, not in title, but in influence. The values I had lived out were now embodied in someone else. That's the truest measure of leadership: not how much you control, but how much of yourself you've multiplied.

It's worth saying this plainly: bad leaders don't clone themselves. They keep their teams dependent because it makes them feel powerful. They stay the smartest person in the room, even if it means progress grinds to a halt without them. Servant leaders do the opposite. They walk with people in the trenches. They model values in real time. They invite others into the work, not to make them followers, but to make them leaders.

Ryan's story is a reminder that when you invest in people deeply, you don't just grow an employee, you grow a carrier of culture. That torch isn't just a metaphor. It's the reality of servant leadership: one life passing fire to another, until the light grows brighter than any one leader could carry alone.

Working Yourself Out of a Job

The hardest truth for many leaders to accept is this: if you do your job well, one day you won't be needed. That's not failure. That's success. Servant leadership isn't about creating dependence, it's about creating strength. It's about building people so capable that the organization no longer rests on your shoulders alone.

When I think back over my years in leadership, some of the most rewarding moments weren't when I was in the spotlight but when I realized the team could carry weight without me. Watching Ryan carry the torch was one example of that. Another came earlier, when we took a risk on hiring a couple of high school kids, sixteen years old, raw talent, and not much else. From the outside, it didn't look like much of an investment. But what they lacked in experience, they made up for in drive. One of them in particular never gave up on himself, and that refusal to quit demanded our investment in return.

Those early years with them weren't glamorous. We were teaching fundamentals while also running a business. But little by little, we walked with them, through deadlines, mistakes, and even personal challenges. We weren't just shaping their work; we were shaping their future. Today, both of them are still in the industry and leading in their own right. That's the payoff of working yourself out of a job: watching the people you once had to lead begin to lead others.

But here's the hard part: once the torch is passed, the responsibility also shifts. Some leaders fear that when they're no longer present to carry the culture of servant leadership, it will fade, and they're not wrong. I've watched things slip in my absence. Servant leaders can only do as much as their own leadership allows. You can plant deeply, you can model faithfully, but you can't guarantee what happens after you leave. That's the tough reality every servant leader must face.

Bad leaders try to solve this by clinging to control. They hold onto their role like it's oxygen, afraid that if someone else steps up, they'll lose their importance. And in doing so, they ensure that everything crumbles the moment they walk away. Servant leaders take a different path. They risk letting go, knowing the culture might not hold perfectly, but believing it's still worth investing, still worth passing on. Because the alternative, never raising anyone else, is far worse.

The Boat Metaphor

Growth is often presented as a ladder, with the leader at the top pulling others up one rung at a time. I've never liked that image. It makes leadership feel like a hierarchy of power, one person above, everyone else below. That isn't how servant leadership works. Leaders don't stand over their teams; they stand with them.

To me, growth is more like a boat.

When you invest in the people around you, it doesn't just raise them individually. It raises the whole boat. Developing people evenly raises the stability of the entire system. A ship riding higher in the water meets less resistance, handles rough seas better, and moves more efficiently toward its destination. That's what shared development does: it reduces drag, lowers error, and creates momentum the organization could never generate if growth were isolated or uneven.

But this is where the metaphor needs honesty. Leaders have to be careful with phrases like, "We're all in the same boat." Because the truth is, sometimes people fall out of the boat, or get pushed out. And when that happens, the question isn't rhetorical. Do you throw them a rope? Do you keep rowing and hope the distance closes on its own? Or do you stop long enough to ask why they went overboard in the first place?

This isn't theoretical for me. My wife and I lived through it.

In a community we loved, one that preached "We're all in the same boat" as a defining identity, conflict hit hard. Decisions were made. Lines were drawn. And before long, we found ourselves outside the very boat we were told we belonged to. We weren't perfect in that season, no one ever is, but we asked for clarity, for accountability, for someone to name what was actually happening.

Instead, leadership chose distance. Not neutrality, self-protection. Telling the truth would have required confronting failures that threatened image and momentum. So rather than engage, they let us drift. We were the safer loss.

That experience marked me. It taught me that good leaders don't avoid conflict when it destabilizes the boat. Servant leadership isn't endless agreeability. It's the courage to set and hold a standard, even when doing so costs you comfort or approval. It's protecting the integrity of the boat and the people in it.

Sometimes people do need to be out of the boat. A team cannot carry unrepentant toxicity or sustained sabotage. But when good people are pushed out unjustly, or when silence allows conflict to fracture trust, the leader's responsibility is clear: create a path back in. Throw the rope. Tell the truth plainly. Do the work required to restore what can be restored.

Because a boat that sheds people through avoidance isn't strong. It's hollow. And hollow boats don't survive rough water.

I've also seen the opposite.

Maritime law carries a simple principle: leave no one behind. Years ago, my wife and I were on a cruise ship in the Caribbean when, in the middle of the night, we were jolted awake by the ship leaning hard to starboard. That doesn't happen on a vessel that size. Later we learned why. The captain had turned the entire ship around to rescue a group of Haitians adrift on a failing raft.

Thousands of passengers were inconvenienced. Schedules were disrupted. None of that mattered. The priority was clear: no one gets left behind.

That moment stayed with me. Leadership isn't only about the people safely on deck. It's about the ones at the edges, the ones at risk of being lost. Good leaders aren't judged by how they treat the strong. They're judged by how they respond to the vulnerable. Sometimes that means slowing the whole ship. Sometimes it means turning it around entirely.

But the message it sends, to everyone watching, is unmistakable.

Takeaways

Carry it Forward

When I look back over my own journey, what stands out the most isn't the projects we shipped, the revenue we generated, or the recognition we earned. It's the people. The teammates who grew into leaders. The young hires who became trusted professionals. The ones who caught the vision of servant leadership and chose to carry it forward. That's the fruit of investment.

No leader is remembered for how much they extracted. They're remembered for how much they invested. Titles fade. Balance sheets change. Companies rise and fall. But the lives you elevate, that legacy doesn't go away. Every hour you give to develop someone, every conversation that sparks confidence, every chance you take on a person who just needs someone to believe in them, all of it adds up to something bigger than yourself.

And here's the reality: investing in people is never efficient. It takes time you don't think you have. It takes resources you sometimes feel like you can't spare. It takes patience when you'd rather just do the work yourself. But it's the only investment that multiplies. It's the only one that pays dividends long after you're gone.

This is why I call it a shared climb. When the people around you rise, so does the organization. When the boat lifts, everyone sails smoother. And when someone falls out, the leader's role is not to row on in silence but to decide how to respond, whether to pull them back in or hold the line. Servant leadership is not soft leadership. It requires courage, clarity, and conviction.

As we turn to the next fundamental, the focus shifts from investment to refinement. If investing in people is how you help them grow, feedback is how you shape that growth. Servant leaders don't just hand people resources and walk away, they walk alongside and say the hard things well. Because the climb isn't just about getting stronger; it's about getting better.

Chapter 18

Trust is the Currency, Earn It Daily

Theology

Leadership rises and falls on trust. You can have vision, strategy, and a plan, but if your people don't trust you, it's all just noise. Without trust, even good ideas feel like a threat. Without trust, standards feel like control. Without trust, change feels like betrayal. Leaders who don't understand this try to compensate with pressure. They push harder, grow louder, or hide behind policy. It doesn't work. When trust is thin, people protect themselves. When trust is strong, they protect the mission. Without it, a team will endure just long enough to find the exit. With it, they'll endure when the pressure hits. With it, they'll move mountains.

In 2023, Gallup studied over 100,000 teams across 122 countries and found one simple truth: trust changes everything. When employees strongly agreed that they trusted their leaders, they were 5.4 times more likely to be engaged and 7 times more likely to say their work had purpose. Teams with low trust reported more burnout, absenteeism, and turnover. That data isn't theory, it's proof that culture rises or falls on relational equity.

When people trust leadership, they stop calculating risk with every decision. Energy once spent on self-protection gets redirected toward performance. It's not a soft concept; it's a measurable productivity gain.

Pocket rule: Where trust grows, resistance shrinks.

Bad leaders try to buy trust with perks, charisma, or authority. Managers try to mandate it with policy and performance plans. Neither works for long. Servant leaders know trust has to be earned, and earned daily.

The Fragility and Cost of Trust

Trust is slow to build and quick to lose. Gallup's research shows engagement rises with trusted leaders, but you don't need a study to see it. When people trust their leaders, they show up differently, more creative, more resilient, more generous.

In two years of data across 180 teams, Google's Project Aristotle reached a simple conclusion: the strongest predictor of team effectiveness wasn't seniority, talent density, or incentives, it was psychological safety (trust made operational). Where safety was high, ideas surfaced earlier, conflict stayed about the work, and teams kept learning instead of hiding mistakes. Subsequent HBR reviews (2022–2024) point in the same direction: teams that report high trust show higher learning behavior and meaningfully better retention over time.

That's what I saw in practice. When trust is present, people stop editing themselves. You get the real signal sooner, what's broken, what's possible, and what needs to change. Progress speeds up because the room isn't wasting energy on self-protection.

Pocket rule: Psychological safety isn't comfort; it's permission to tell the truth.

When that trust erodes, everything contracts. It gets smaller. People default to self-preservation. They stop taking risks. They only do what's required. Then predictably, the organization adds more oversight, more turnover, more missed opportunities.

That's why I never assumed trust was automatic. It didn't matter how long someone had worked with me or how many wins we had behind us, trust still had to be earned in the present tense. Not banked on the past. Not borrowed against the future. Earned now. One choice, one decision, one interaction, one conversation at a time.

Stories

Daily Deposits

For me, those deposits weren't complicated. They looked like showing up early and staying late without making a scene about it. They looked like answering questions honestly the first time they were asked, then answering them again when someone needed to hear it differently.

A 2023 Harvard Business Review analysis of forty-two organizations tracked how leaders built or lost credibility over time. The clearest signal wasn't empathy or inspiration, it was follow-through. When employees strongly agreed that their leaders "did what they said they would do," engagement scores were 38 percent higher, and voluntary turnover fell by nearly half over twelve months. The pattern held across industries and pay scales.

Consistency is the quiet proof of integrity. Every kept promise deposits confidence into the account you lead from. Every missed one withdraws more than words can repay. That's why trust is rarely rebuilt with a speech, it's rebuilt with repetition.

Pocket rule: Trust compounds through repetition, not revelation.

They looked like writing things on the whiteboard where everyone could see them, priorities, timelines, responsibilities, and standing there long enough to make sure silence didn't hide confusion.

We also made it tangible. Lunches catered in once a week, breakfast drop-ins on busy project days, and an open-door policy that wasn't just a phrase. It was the whole posture: be interruptible. Be present. If I had to choose between a perfect plan and a present leader, I'd choose presence every time. People didn't trust me because of the perks, but because the culture had become magnetic.

But the real deposits weren't in breakfasts or Friday happy hours. They were in the small, quiet moments that no one posts on social media. A late-night text was answered. A hard conversation handled with dignity. A correction made in private and an affirmation given in public. We had those moments on repeat. We respected the room. We let the coach have the floor. We laid out standards when it was time and then got out of the way so people could work. And we celebrated, supported, or carried the weight of every one of those moments as a team.

And we grieved together too. The deepest test of trust came when we lost one of our own.

Sevie was my project, my right hand in the design world, and my friend. She died too young, and it ripped a hole in all of us. She was brave, talented, and honest. She made me better and kept me honest. I loved who she was. Even though she's gone, I still do. Her life and her loss shaped the way I lead. That's part of why I carry her with me in the tattoo on my arm with her favorite phrase: "Wage War."

Moments like these are where trust either fractures or forges. Ours forged. I didn't have to pretend I was strong. I didn't have to perform. We showed up for each other. We were present. The work continued because the work had purpose, not in spite of the loss, but because our trust was already deep. And in the aftermath, it only grew deeper.

I hesitate to call it family, because that word is thrown around too easily in business. It can become a manipulative way to demand loyalty without earning it. What we had was different. Trust pulled the best out of people and helped them rise. Some stayed, others carried what they learned into new seasons of their lives. That was never a loss to me, it was the point. We built a place where standards were high, grace was higher, and growth was the natural outcome of people being trusted to develop at their own pace and in their own direction.

At scale, that language has to shift. I only had 104 people at our largest, so we could still build trust through presence. In larger organizations, you need rituals and systems that carry trust beyond proximity. At that point, the leader's job is to turn personal posture into a cultural expectation, not just the owner's personal posture.

And this doesn't fall only on leaders. Employees carry responsibility too. If you want to be trusted, be trustworthy. Deliver on time. Communicate clearly. Own your misses. Don't hide behind the "that's above my pay grade" line. Don't choose the easy path of cynicism or gossip. Don't protect yourself at all costs. That posture is a trust-killer.

For those who want to lead, even if they don't have the title yet: make deposits first. Carry weight that isn't yours yet. Be the one who goes first. Trust travels both directions when people live like that. And it can be built. It is possible on both sides, no matter the size of the company.

The result was a team that ran hot without burning out. Pressure didn't scatter us; it bonded us. We weren't perfect, but we were in it together, and they wanted to be part of the climb.

The Trust Ledger

I never sat down with a spreadsheet or a notebook to track credibility. That's not how it works. Trust isn't math. It isn't accounting. It isn't a game you keep score on.

The ledger was lived. People were counting, even when I wasn't. They noticed if my yes stayed yes. They noticed if I showed up when I said I would. They noticed that if I gave the same standard to everyone instead of protecting favorites.

Every leader has a ledger, whether they acknowledge it or not. It's written in the minds of the people who experience you. Every action is either a deposit or a withdrawal.

MIT Sloan's 2023 Trust Repair in Leadership study followed 2,500 employees through organizational crises and found that leaders who acknowledged failure quickly and took visible corrective action restored trust six times faster than those who minimized or deflected blame. The mechanism wasn't an apology alone, it was transparency paired with consistent behavior afterward.

Trust doesn't just live in success; it's proven in recovery. People don't expect perfection, they expect truth followed by movement. Every time you face a hard moment honestly, you make a deposit in someone's confidence that you'll handle the next one the same way.

Pocket rule: Honesty repairs what silence breaks.

Withdrawals happen, silence, delay, inconsistency, pride. What separates leaders isn't perfection. It's honesty. When trust leaks, do you surface it fast? Do you repair it? Or do you pretend it didn't happen?

The Trust Ledger is just a way of naming what was already happening. It wasn't a tool I carried. It was the natural log of whether people could count on me, day in and day out.

Withdrawals and Repair

Trust doesn't just depend on the deposits you make. It's also about how you handle withdrawals when they inevitably happen. Missing a deadline without acknowledging it is a withdrawal. Making a decision that surprises the team because you didn't communicate early is a withdrawal. Failing to apply the same standard to your favorites that you apply to everyone else is a withdrawal. People will forgive a lot when they trust you. What they won't forgive is dishonesty, favoritism, or pride.

Repair is the hard part. It's also the place where trust often grows the most. You repair by telling the truth. You repair by naming exactly what happened and why. You repair by apologizing without qualification and then fixing the process that let it happen. You repair by recommitting to the standard, not just to the relationship.

I learned that backing leaders in public and correcting in private was the best way to reduce withdrawals. It preserved dignity and reinforced alignment. When something blew up online, I shut down public chatter and handled it privately with the person involved. Then I showed up in the room and explained the standard again. Not louder, just clearer.

When it was my miss, I said so. That mattered as much as anything. People don't need a perfect leader; they need an honest one.

And trust doesn't just create stability, it accelerates growth. When a team fully trusts each other, the speed of decision-making increases. Accountability becomes shared rather than policed. People start to anticipate needs instead of waiting to be told. And when people anticipate, they start solving problems before they become fires. That's the kind of organization that outlasts talent gaps and market swings. It becomes antifragile because its foundation isn't dependent on one hero. It's built on a thousand kept promises.

Trust also reduces the cost of operations. When people believe you, you don't need as many approvals, as many meetings, or as much redundant oversight. The energy you save from arguing and defending can be spent on building.

Deloitte's 2022 Human Capital Trends report found that organizations described by their own employees as "high-trust ecosystems" made decisions 30 percent faster and delivered strategic initiatives 40 percent more effectively than peers with low trust. The gain wasn't from working longer hours, it came from cutting friction.

Bureaucracy is what grows in the absence of belief. Every approval chain or redundant meeting is a hedge against someone's doubt. Remove that friction and people move without waiting for permission. The energy that once fueled defense now fuels progress.

Pocket rule: Speed is the dividend of trust.

Trust takes time to earn, but once it compounds, it pays for itself every day.

There is also a cost to losing it. Losing trust increases churn. It pushes your best people to the edges. It steals creativity and slows momentum. Losing even one key person can set a company back months.

I saw the power of trust firsthand with Kahlie. I'd known of her as a high school student with my boys, and fresh out of college I hired her to help me build and lead our project management team. We were starting from scratch, and the pressure was immense. The pace we had to sustain wasn't forgiving, and we hit wall after wall trying to create a structure that could carry the weight of the work.

Kahlie was wired for detail. She loved processes and documentation, where I had to work harder at them. That difference could have turned into friction, but trust kept it from breaking down. We had some intense conversations, disagreements about path and approach, but there was mutual respect in every one of them. I trusted her enough to let her build. She trusted me enough to tell me when the system needed to change. We both stayed under the standard. We argued for the work, not for our egos. We shared the same aim: build a team that could carry others.

Within a couple of months, we had the structure. In a year, we had a strong department. And Kahlie had grown from an entry-level hire to a leader with a voice that changed the company. It was a steep climb from graduation to leadership, and she earned every step.

That's what trust makes possible. It doesn't just create harmony; it creates momentum. It opens doors that policies can't. It empowers people to run faster because they know you won't pull the rug out from under them. It's how we built a department where none existed and launched a young leader into her calling.

And the return doesn't stop when the job ends. Years later, I still carry pride for the people who came through our doors and outgrew us. That's the right outcome. That's the point. If you do this right, the trust you build outlasts your brand because it was never about the brand. It was always about the bond.

Takeaway

Now, can every leader personally maintain this kind of connection at scale? No. As you grow, you can't be everywhere at once. But you can extend trust by raising up other leaders who carry the same convictions. You can codify standards so the culture protects itself. You can create rhythms where trust is taught, measured by outcomes, and reinforced.

That doesn't mean creating clones in personality or style. Diversity of thought and approach is the strength of a healthy team. It means alignment in values and standards, between teammates, clients, vendors, and the wider community.

When that's in place, trust compounds. It becomes the kind of return every business actually wants, return on relationship that shows up in quality, retention, and reputation. It's the kind of revenue you get to choose: not revenue that fades, but relationships that remain.

At the end of the day, trust is the real currency of leadership. And once you've earned it, you have a responsibility to spend it on the right things: clarity, courage, and standards that free people to reach their potential. Say the hard thing because you love them, not because you're right. That's the next layer. And that's where this book goes next, because the real climb continues when leaders say the hard things well.

Chapter 19

Feedback Fuels Growth, Say the Hard Things Well

Theology

The Hardest Part of Leadership

The hardest thing I've ever done as a leader wasn't carrying the financial risk of payroll. It wasn't the long hours or even the constant uncertainty of the market. Those things were heavy, but they never matched the weight of looking another human being in the eye and saying, "This isn't right."

Correction is the crucible of leadership. If you're serious about growth, you can't avoid it. A team that never hears honest feedback will eventually stall out. Mistakes repeat. Blind spots turn into fractures. Frustration grows silently until it poisons the culture. That's why good leaders never dodge the hard conversations.

Gallup's 2023 State of the Global Workplace study found that employees who receive meaningful feedback at least weekly are 3.2 times more likely to be engaged and 2.7 times more likely to strongly trust their manager. The same data set showed that lack of feedback ranked among the top three predictors of voluntary turnover.

Feedback isn't friction; it's fuel. When people know where they stand, they stop wasting energy guessing. The conversation might sting, but it anchors belonging instead of eroding it.

Pocket rule: Silence kills more progress than conflict ever could.

I didn't have to sit down for hard conversations every day. In fact, good leadership usually prevents a lot of conflict from ever reaching that point. But when those conversations did come, I didn't dodge them. Almost every time, I opened with the same line: "This is going to be a hard one." I didn't say it for drama. I said it to set the agenda before we ever got into the details. No surprises. No buildup of tension. Just clarity: this was going to be difficult, but it was also going to be honest.

Google's Re: Work program confirmed that teams with leaders who frame difficult feedback conversations in advance, clarity before criticism, score 35 percent higher in psychological safety and resolve performance issues 60 percent faster. When people know what's coming, the brain's threat response drops. They can hear correction as care instead of an attack.

Hard truth, named early, preserves dignity on both sides. It tells the other person, "You're safe here, even when it's uncomfortable." That's leadership under pressure, not performance under the spotlight.

Pocket rule: Clarity is kindness under tension.

Feedback, when it's real, feels like standing in a blacksmith's forge. The metal doesn't get stronger without fire and hammering. Sparks fly. The heat is uncomfortable. But the process produces strength that can withstand pressure. Without the forge, the steel stays weak. Without correction, people stay fragile in their blind spots.

A 2022 MIT Sloan study tracking 1,800 managers showed that teams receiving direct, behavior-specific feedback improved measurable output by 19 percent in six months compared with peers relying on annual reviews. The same research found that performance dips only when feedback is vague or delayed.

Precision builds trust. Generalities build confusion. The forge analogy holds: the heat refines, not destroys, when you keep it focused.

Pocket rule: Specific beats soft every time.

It's also like holding up a mirror. Nobody sees themselves clearly without one. Leaders aren't punishing when they give feedback, they're reflecting. They're offering a view of reality that someone can't see on their own.

Deloitte's 2023 Human Capital Trends report found that employees who described post-feedback follow-up from leaders as "consistent and fair" were 4.6 times more likely to report high trust levels six months later. It isn't the correction that breaks trust; it's abandonment afterward.

Great leaders circle back. They check progress, reinforce wins, and remind the person why the hard talk happened in the first place, because they matter. That second conversation deposits what the first one withdrew.

Pocket rule: Follow-up is the final word in feedback.

And if you've ever been part of sports, you know the point. No athlete in history improved without correction. They don't just practice; they train. Training means a coach calls out bad form, shows a better way, and demands repetition until it sticks. Work is no different. If we want our people to grow, we have to be willing to coach.

The hardest part of leadership isn't the spreadsheets or the strategy. It's choosing to walk into the forge with another person, knowing the sparks will fly, but also believing the strength on the other side is worth it.

Truth as Service, Not a Weapon

Not all feedback builds strength. I've seen leaders swing truth like a hammer, determined to crush mistakes and remind everyone who's in charge. Those conversations don't produce growth; they produce fear. And fear never creates excellence. At best, it produces compliance, people who do just enough to stay out of trouble but never bring their best selves to the table.

It gets worse when leaders manufacture their own version of truth and wield that instead. I've watched leaders invent problems, exaggerate mistakes, or slap unfair labels on people to maintain control. That isn't correction, it's abuse. It's not about building up the person in front of them; it's about protecting ego or inflating authority. And when people see that kind of behavior, they don't just lose respect for the leader. They lose trust in the entire system. If truth can be twisted once, it can be twisted again. No one feels safe in a culture like that.

I've seen the opposite mistake too, leaders so afraid of conflict that they sugarcoat everything. They soften the message, circle around the issue, or drown it in vague encouragement until the point is lost. That doesn't create safety; it creates confusion. People deserve clarity, not half-truths dressed up to avoid discomfort.

Servant leadership takes a different path. It pairs truth with care. It delivers clarity without cruelty. It puts the person first and the problem second. When I walked into hard conversations, my goal wasn't to prove I was right or to defend my authority. My goal was to help us move forward.

That's why I've always preferred to say, "We work together," instead of, "You work for me." Some might call it a small thing, but I believe it matters. It reframes the relationship. It levels the ground. When feedback comes from someone who positions themselves as with you instead of over you, trust rises. And when trust is present, even the hardest words can be received as a gift instead of an attack.

Truth, when it's delivered this way, becomes an act of service. It clears the fog. It calls people up instead of tearing them down. It builds confidence instead of destroying it. It reminds the entire team that leadership isn't about being right, it's about doing right by the people you lead.

Stories

Owning Your Part First

I never walked into a correction conversation assuming I was the problem. That wouldn't have helped anyone. But I did make a habit of asking myself first: Did I contribute to this?

Sometimes the answer was yes. Maybe I hadn't been clear, maybe priorities were stacked wrong, or maybe I hadn't given someone the support they needed. Most of the time the responsibility sat primarily with the individual, but I didn't want to ignore the possibility that leadership had played a role too.

So when I sat down with someone, I tried to leave space for that. I didn't dramatize it or beat myself up, I just talked like a human. If I had dropped the ball, I admitted it. If I hadn't, I stayed focused on the issue at hand. The point wasn't to take blame that didn't belong to me. The point was to make sure the conversation was about the whole picture, not just one side of it.

What I found is that when leaders show they're willing to own their part, even in small ways, people become far more willing to own theirs. It shifts the conversation from defensiveness to problem-solving. Instead of a standoff, it becomes a joint effort to fix what went wrong and make it better the next time.

Leaders who can't do that usually fall into the opposite trap. They come in looking to assign blame, assuming laziness or malice when most of the time it's just misalignment. They want to win the moment instead of fixing the issue. And they end up standing alone, because nobody trusts a leader who always has to be right.

Servant leadership doesn't assume guilt, but it does allow for humility. It recognizes that leadership can contribute to failure and that owning that part, when it's real, builds trust. That balance, not groveling, not excusing, but staying honest, is what makes correction safe enough to spark growth.

Grace + Forward Momentum

Correction, by itself, doesn't accomplish much. If all you do is point out what went wrong, people walk away discouraged, or worse, defensive. Feedback only becomes leadership when it points forward. That's why almost every hard conversation I had followed the same rhythm: set the agenda, name the problem, and then move quickly into a plan for what comes next.

I knew the pace we were working at. It wasn't rocket science, but it was close. Deadlines were tight, expectations were high, and the margin for error was small. Chaos came with the territory. In that kind of environment, finger-pointing was useless. What people needed most was clarity, what to fix, how to fix it, and the confidence that they weren't walking alone.

That's where grace mattered. Grace didn't mean lowering the bar or excusing failure. It meant I approached the conversation with awareness. I understood the pressures, the fatigue, the reality that mistakes often came from confusion or overload, not malice or laziness. Grace gave people the freedom to be honest about what went wrong without fear of being crushed for it.

But grace alone isn't enough. Pair it with accountability, and you create momentum. Once the problem was on the table, the focus turned to solutions: What needs to change? How do we make sure it doesn't happen again? What resources or clarity are missing? The energy shifted from blame to progress.

Research backs this up. Gallup reports that employees who receive meaningful feedback weekly are nearly three times more engaged than those who don't. Other studies show organizations with strong feedback cultures see turnover drop by double digits. These numbers aren't just statistics, they confirm what we saw every day: feedback delivered with grace and clarity strengthens commitment instead of eroding it.

Some leaders miss this balance. They lean too hard on accountability, turning feedback into punishment. Others lean only on grace, softening every issue until nothing changes. Servant leadership demands both. Truth delivered with care. Standards held with empathy. A clear plan laid out with the confidence that we'll get there together.

That rhythm, agenda, problem, path forward, wasn't just a method for me. It was how I protected the culture. It reminded everyone that mistakes weren't the end of the story. Growth was still possible. Trust was still intact. The work still mattered, and so did they.

Takeaways

The Cultural Payoff

When feedback is delivered with clarity, grace, and accountability, the payoff shows up everywhere. It shows up in trust, in performance, and in the kind of culture that makes people excited to come to work.

I saw it firsthand. My team wasn't afraid of feedback, they expected it. They knew it wasn't going to be random, petty, or manipulative. They knew correction would be honest and direct, and it would always come with a path forward. That predictability gave us the ability to run hot without burning out. People didn't waste energy protecting themselves. They poured it into solving problems and advancing the work.

That's why the crying couch became a symbol in our office. People knew they could sit down, tell me anything, from personal struggles to work-related mistakes, and it would be safe. Feedback wasn't just about performance. It was about creating a place where people could bring their whole selves, knowing they wouldn't be dismissed or destroyed for it. That kind of psychological safety freed people to be bold in the work and honest in the struggle.

The payoff showed up in loyalty too. My team wasn't just compliant; they were committed. They trusted me enough to run hard, because they knew I wasn't going to blindside them with hidden expectations or punish them for being human. They knew correction wasn't about taking them down, it was about building them up.

The research echoes what we lived. Gallup has shown that organizations where employees strongly agree their manager provides meaningful feedback see nearly three times the level of engagement compared to those where feedback is rare. Harvard Business Review has documented that feedback-rich cultures are also more innovative, because people aren't afraid to speak up. And MIT Sloan points out that psychological safety is one of the strongest predictors of high-performing teams.

Leaders who try to "win" every interaction end up alone. Their people avoid them, hide from them, or eventually leave. But leaders who treat feedback as service, who deliver it with clarity, humility, and care, build teams that last. They don't just extract effort; they multiply it. They don't just protect themselves; they protect the culture. And they create environments where people don't just work hard, they work with heart.

That's the cultural payoff of feedback done well. It's not just better performance, it's stronger trust, deeper loyalty, and a team that's willing to climb the shared mountain with you. And that, at the end of the day, is the whole point of servant leadership: not to stand at the top of the hill alone, but to reach the summit together.

Chapter 20

Feedback Ecosystem, Truth in Every Direction

Theology

Truth Is a System, Not a Speech

When you're shoulder to shoulder with a handful of people, feedback happens naturally. You're in the same room, solving the same problems, and it's easy to spot when something's off. Growth changes that. As soon as your team expands beyond daily proximity, truth starts to scatter. Leaders can't possibly keep everything front of mind. At scale, feedback doesn't just need courage, it needs structure.

Gallup's 2023 State of the Manager study found that organizations with structured feedback systems, scheduled 1-on-1s, peer loops, and upward reviews reported 31 percent higher engagement and 24 percent fewer quality defects than those relying on ad-hoc conversations. Scale doesn't kill truth; missing systems do.

A healthy structure doesn't replace courage, it preserves it. It keeps information moving even when proximity fades, ensuring people far from the center still feel seen and accountable.

Pocket rule: Build rails before you build reach.

I hated walking into a conversation only to be reminded of something I should have caught but didn't. At a relentless pace, that fear of missing something critical never went away. Without systems, the leader becomes the weak link, reacting instead of leading.

That's why feedback has to be more than a one-off conversation. It has to be an ecosystem where truth flows in every direction: downward, so leaders sharpen their people; upward, so teams can correct their leaders; sideways, so peers can challenge each other without it being mistaken for rebellion.

Deloitte's 2022 Human Capital Trends survey found that companies enabling upward feedback, where employees can critique leadership decisions safely, were 12 times more likely to report high organizational trust. When truth only travels down, it becomes compliance; when it travels up, it becomes culture.

Inviting correction doesn't weaken authority, it legitimizes it. People don't expect leaders to be flawless; they expect them to be reachable.

Pocket rule: Invite the mirror before it finds you.

Servant leadership sees truth as a shared asset, not the possession of the leader. When truth is hoarded at the top, it becomes distorted and weaponized. But when truth flows freely, it becomes a resource everyone can use to align decisions, correct mistakes, and build trust. Truth belongs to the team. The leader's job is not to control it but to distribute it. That's why feedback systems aren't optional, they're stewardship.

MIT Sloan's 2023 Leading in Networks research showed that teams operating with open-data, multi-directional feedback networks delivered 22 percent faster project cycles and 34 percent higher cross-department trust. Transparency created speed because everyone was solving from the same reality.

That's the quiet math of stewardship: the more you share truth, the less energy is wasted reconciling versions of it.

Pocket rule: Shared truth moves faster than managed truth.

Stories

Making Feedback Routine

As the company grew, I had to admit something: I couldn't keep it all in my head anymore. In the early days, I knew what every designer and developer was working on. I could catch problems in real time because I was in the room when they happened. But with more people came more moving parts, and hallway conversations weren't enough.

What forced the change was realizing feedback couldn't be left to chance. If it didn't have a predictable cadence, it got buried under deadlines. We needed set places where the truth could surface, where it wasn't threatening or rare, but expected.

So we built steady patterns. One-on-ones gave space for both wins and struggles before they snowballed. Team reviews allowed us to look back honestly at what went right and what needed to change. Larger check-ins kept everyone rowing in the same direction. It wasn't glamorous, but it gave feedback a home.

Predictability was the key. When feedback had a rhythm, the fear drained out of it. People didn't wonder if being pulled aside meant they were in trouble. They knew refinement was part of how we worked. For me, it relieved the dread of realizing too late that something had been slipping by unnoticed.

And there's another reality: as a leader, there comes a point where you're no longer directly connected to the work, or, in my case, sometimes the work itself was over my head. I had engineers building things I couldn't evaluate on my own. In those moments, feedback wasn't just about coaching them; it was a lifeline for me. Without those rhythms, I would have been blind to both the progress and the problems.

The research backs this up. Zenger Folkman found that leaders who frequently ask for feedback are rated significantly higher in effectiveness. PwC reports that nearly 60% of employees want feedback either daily or weekly, not annually. The very thing leaders fear people will resist is what they're quietly hoping for. Rhythm builds trust. It proves people's voices won't vanish into a black hole; they'll be heard regularly and with the intent to act.

The Challenger's Seat, Dissent as Duty

Most leaders say they want honesty, but what they really mean is feedback that doesn't sting. The test comes when someone pushes back in a way that feels like defiance.

I'll never forget one situation where an employee looked like he was flat-out refusing to do his job. From the outside, it seemed like negligence, even insubordination. I was told to fire him. Instead, I sat down to hear his side. What surfaced wasn't laziness, it was a pattern of misalignment between what had been promised and what was being asked of him. His "no" wasn't rebellion; it was courage to draw a line where we hadn't yet. Had I ended his journey without listening, we would have lost a good man and failed to see the deeper truth.

That experience reinforced something for me: leaders need dissent. But they also need to know how to respond when it shows up. If dissent is punished, people go silent. They stop raising concerns, stop pointing out risks, and stop telling the truth. Silence isn't loyalty; it's retreat. And when the room goes quiet, the leader's blind spots grow wider until the whole team is in danger.

I saw a model of the right response long before I was in leadership. My father's students used to talk about how he confronted problems. He never yelled or raised his voice. He got quieter. More focused. He drew students in close, and in that calm, they felt the weight of what he said. It was as if he were imprinting the truth directly on their hearts. That kind of authority didn't create fear, it created respect.

But dissent has boundaries. Not every pushback is constructive. Some people use "speaking their mind" as a cover for whining or as a crutch to avoid owning their performance. That's not dissent, that's avoidance. The difference is fairness. Real dissent names what's broken and points toward a better way. Whining only names the problem to justify staying stuck.

Some leaders swing to the other extreme, treating every challenge as an attack. For them, authority is absolute, never to be questioned. Speak up and you've marked yourself for retribution. Grudges get held. Careers get quietly sabotaged. In those environments, asking a hard question is the same as signing your exit papers. The result isn't loyalty; it's fear. Leaders like that may get compliance, but they'll never earn commitment.

The research bears this out. Amy Edmondson's work on psychological safety shows that teams with space for dissent consistently outperform those without it. Those teams aren't making more mistakes, they're just willing to talk about them. That willingness leads to faster learning, better performance, and stronger outcomes.

Servant leadership doesn't see dissent as rebellion. It sees it as a duty, and it responds with curiosity, not retaliation. Because in those moments when truth feels threatening, the leader's reaction decides whether trust deepens or dies.

Piercing the Bubble, Upward Feedback

One of the most dangerous dynamics in leadership is the bubble. The higher you climb, the less unfiltered truth reaches you. People hesitate to tell the boss what's really happening, especially if the news is bad. Even well-meaning employees filter their words. The result is that leaders can feel informed while actually being blind.

I lived this tension early on. As the work got more complex and technical, I found myself in over my head. My engineers were making decisions I couldn't always evaluate. If communication wasn't clear or complete, I had no way of knowing. Feedback from them wasn't optional, it was my compass back to reality.

Most organizations never build safe ways for truth to travel upward. People learn to tell leaders what they want to hear, not what they need to know. That's why leaders have to create intentional structures. For me, that meant making time to sit down with people all across the company, not just my direct reports. It meant creating space for pushback and showing I could handle negative feedback when it was fair and constructive. I relied on surveys and one-on-ones to keep a pulse on the culture, and we worked hard to build an environment where people felt safe telling the truth upward.

The research confirms how critical this is. A 2021 MIT Sloan Management Review study found that leaders consistently rate themselves much higher on openness than their employees do. That gap is a warning sign: the bubble is real. SHRM estimates that workplace silence and miscommunication cost organizations over half a trillion dollars annually in lost productivity. Harvard Business Review also shows that weak upward feedback loops correlate with higher turnover and "toxic" Glassdoor ratings. Silence isn't neutral; it's expensive.

Servant leadership requires humility here. You can't just say, "My door is always open." That's passive leadership. You have to go first, invite the feedback, protect the people who give it, and show what you did with it. Otherwise, silence will take over, and silence is deadly.

The best leaders pierce their own bubble before it hardens. They don't just ask for upward feedback once; they normalize it, systematize it, and respond to it in public. When people see their words change something, they'll keep telling you the truth. And truth, especially upward truth, is what keeps leaders from drifting into arrogance or irrelevance.

Takeaways

Practical Playbook, Building the Ecosystem

The beauty of a feedback ecosystem is that it scales. It doesn't matter if you're leading twenty people or two hundred, the principles hold. The question is whether you'll be intentional enough to design it instead of leaving truth to chance.

For owners:

Put predictable rhythms in place. One-on-ones, team reviews, and quarterly check-ins aren't luxuries, they're lifelines. Protect time for them even when the pace is brutal. Make upward feedback a structural part of the business, not a suggestion.

For mid-level leaders:

Protect the lane for dissent. Don't let it turn into endless complaint sessions, but don't squash it either. When people raise concerns, respond with calm curiosity. Model the posture of your leadership so your team knows pushback won't end their career.

For aspiring leaders:

Practice receiving feedback without defensiveness. Show that you can handle truth, even when it stings. The earlier you build that muscle, the more trust you'll earn. Leaders who can't receive feedback won't be trusted to give it.

And one final discipline for every level: close the loop. When people give feedback and never hear what happened with it, cynicism sets in. Even if the answer is "not now," leaders owe their teams a response. Closing the loop proves that truth is valued, not just collected. Without it, feedback becomes noise. With it, feedback becomes fuel.

The thread through all of this is simple: feedback has to be a practice, not a reaction. When it's predictable, honest, and fair, it strengthens the culture instead of weakening it. That's how you move from feedback as an event to feedback as an ecosystem.

Chapter 21

The Shield & the Mirror

Theology

Why this matters

Leadership asks two things at once: stand between harm and the people who rely on you, and be honest about whether you can still stand there. The first is the shield, an outward act of protection, standard enforcement, and public defense. The second is the mirror, an inward act of scrutiny, ownership, and a willingness to step back when capacity runs out. Both are required. One without the other becomes martyrdom or desertion.

Harvard Business Review's 2023 global leadership resilience study tracked 2,700 senior leaders over two years and found that those who practiced "dual accountability", balancing personal reflection with external advocacy, retained their teams at a rate 47 percent higher than those who focused only on performance protection. The research confirmed what most frontline leaders already sense: the moment the shield never meets the mirror, burnout follows.

Protection without reflection becomes pride. Reflection without protection becomes paralysis. Servant leadership stands in the tension between both, anchored, transparent, and human.

Pocket rule: A leader's first shield is honesty about their own limits.

This isn't theory. It's operational. The shield creates a safe field where people can do the work without being ground down by noise, politics, or petty cruelty. The mirror keeps leaders from turning that defense into self-destructive pride. A steward who cannot see their limits destroys both himself and the thing he intended to protect.

Gallup's 2023 Workplace Resilience Index surveyed more than 15,000 managers across 36 countries and found that teams whose leaders explicitly state personal capacity and model boundary-setting report 44 percent lower burnout and 29 percent higher sustained performance over twelve months. The research echoed what this section names as stewardship: protection that scales only when limits are known.

Capacity isn't a confession of weakness; it's an operating standard. When leaders normalize that truth, accountability stops feeling punitive and starts feeling shared.

Pocket rule: Model limits before the work models you.

Put plainly, culture dies when leaders refuse to protect it; culture also dies when leaders keep protecting it at the cost of their health, judgment, and moral authority. Servant leadership is the practical work of managing that tension: enforce standards, protect dignity, and keep checking whether you can reasonably carry the load. If you can't, the humane, strategic, move is to slow, delegate, or rebuild the shield with others.

Harvard Business Review's 2023 Adaptive Leadership Under Pressure report found that organizations where leaders share protective responsibility, through delegation, peer guardians, or distributed authority, maintain operational stability 37 percent longer during crises than those centered on a single "heroic" leader. The findings reinforce what this section teaches: sustainability is a team function, not an individual virtue.

Sacrifice, when planned and distributed, multiplies strength. When hoarded, it drains the very culture it was meant to save.

Pocket rule: Shared shields don't crack as easily.

Stories

The Mirror

In 2021 a nurse practitioner pulled my wife aside, with my permission, and said, "Look." He laid my labs on the table. They weren't borderline. They were objectively bad. If health could be read like a calendar, he pointed to the day my body would fail if nothing changed.

That was not a cinematic conversion. It was a factual, clinical alarm. For years I had lived like the bottle behind me was endless. The gym, the software work, the church obligations, family, I had treated all of it as fires I could always put out. The labs were a blunt instrument that proved otherwise.

That mirror moment forced a reframing. Stewardship isn't only about taking on more for people you love. It is also about being able to hold the center over time. If the steward collapses, the center collapses with him. From that day, I began measuring every big ask against a single question: Can I physically and mentally hold what I'm about to take on? If the honest answer was no, the right moves were delegation, a pause, or exit. That was not surrender; it was triage.

A 2022 MIT Sloan Management Review longitudinal study on executive burnout found that leaders who instituted capacity audits, scheduled reviews of workload, energy, and recovery, reduced leadership turnover by 42 percent and improved team performance scores by 18 percent within a year. The reason was simple: when the center holds, everything around it steadies.

Longevity isn't luck; it's measured stewardship. A healthy leader sustains the mission longer than a heroic one ever could.

Pocket rule: Rest is the discipline that protects purpose.

I should be clear: knowing the answer and living it are different things. The clarity I gained in that clinic didn't become practice overnight, I lived with the idea for years before it truly landed. It took until January of 2025 for me to fully accept what the labs had meant. I was buried in the mess. Don't be like me: having a diagnosis doesn't automatically change habits.

That mirror also changed how I thought about public defense. If I were going to step into the gap for others, I had to be sure I would still be able to stand there later. That meant choosing fights with more strategy, what I would take on, what I would hand off, and what I would contain with policy rather than personal energy. Leadership longevity is tactical, not romantic.

The Shield

When the gym teetered toward failure, stepping in to protect it was not heroic theater. It was a service. It wasn't my dream; it was a friend's. But the coaches, the members, the neighborhood, those people needed that place to exist. So I chose to stand between the threat and them.

That season was a composite of the ordinary, costly things a shield does. We covered payroll shortfalls. We fixed vendor tangles. I answered member texts at odd hours and showed up to classes when coaches couldn't. We backed coaches in public and handled the corrective work privately. Those thousand small actions show up, answer the call, stand in the doorway, and keep the room alive long enough for better systems to begin to take root.

Protection meant accepting visible cost. It meant taking blame, absorbing friction, and accepting that preserving dignity in the moment sometimes makes you unpopular elsewhere. It meant enforcing standards evenly, even when doing so was the harder path politically. When public blow-ups threatened the space, we shut down the noise, addressed the issue directly with those involved, and then returned to the floor to restate the standard. Quiet correction, loud support, that rhythm stabilized the room.

The cost was real and compound. There was the immediate financial cost, stabilizing payroll, stepping in to cover shortfalls, and occasionally fronting vendor or repair expenses to keep the doors open. There was the relational cost, missed family dinners, delayed vacations, and the strain on daily rhythms for Carie and the kids. There was the health cost, sleep lost and stress compounded on a body that was already compromised. And there was the opportunity cost, time and money diverted from other initiatives that might have grown our work without the same degree of personal exposure.

All of those costs required hard accounting. Not in a spreadsheet for the reader, but in reality: how long could we keep absorbing before the shield itself broke? That's the question leaders rarely like to answer, but it's the most strategic one you'll face when protection is required.

Deloitte's 2023 Human Capital Trends report found that leaders who performed regular "capacity audits" of time, budget, and well-being were 2.4 times more likely to sustain organizational trust through financial stress and 30 percent more likely to meet strategic goals on schedule. The point wasn't bookkeeping, it was clarity. When leaders stay honest about what protection actually requires, they make decisions that strengthen both the people they serve and the structure that supports them.

Servant leadership doesn't hide the bill; it pays it openly so others learn what the work really costs.

Pocket rule: Unmeasured costs become unintended losses.

This was a callback to the mirror. The labs from 2021 didn't vanish; they were part of every decision I made while defending the place in 2023. Protection only worked when paired with honest self-assessment. Without that balance, the effort either collapsed from overextension or stalled from hesitation. That is the hard mechanical work of stewardship, enacting protection while managing capacity.

Takeaways

Where posture becomes practice, lessons learned the hard way

These are not elegant mandates. They are blunt, tactical moves I learned by failing first and fixing later. I include them here so you can skip some of the bruises.

- State your capacity explicitly. If you plan to shield, tell people what you can and cannot carry. Limits remove guesswork and resentment. Example lines that worked for us: "I will handle vendor disputes and payroll triage; I will not own day-to-day class schedules." Saying that didn't eliminate work; it removed resentment and clarified who had authority to act.

- Defend publicly; correct privately. Stand with your people in front of the room, restate the standard and remove immediate heat. Do the corrective work behind closed doors so the person keeps dignity. The effect is immediate: a coach feels supported; the room calms; the problem gets solved with less collateral damage.

- Raise and protect deputies. A shield that cannot be shared is brittle. Identify people who can be trained to stand where you stand. In Carthage, pivoting programming and operations to Brock was one of those moves: it moved responsibility to someone who could carry day-to-day presence more sustainably. Promote people into the shield, then protect them when they take heat. That protection is often the leader's most valuable work.

- Make repair direct, not theatrical. When you miss or withdraw trust, fix it plainly. Name the miss. Apologize where required. Change the process that allowed it. We found that short, honest repairs deposited more credibility than grand public mea culpas. Repair needs to restore function, not earn applause.

- Triage your fights. Not every problem deserves your shield. Ask whether the issue is systemic, relational, or performative. If systemic, fix the system. If relational, counsel and repair. If performative, contain and move on. Save steward energy for the fights that truly protect people.

- Track the cost. Every act of protection has a cost. Track the human cost (sleep, family strain), the financial cost (out-of-pocket support), and the reputational cost (taking blame publicly). That tracking is less about metrics and more about honest limits, how many nights of sleep can you trade before the product of your leadership is damaged?

- Lean on counsel and accountability. When the mess becomes personal and legal, lean on counsel and on the board you've assembled for accountability, not for theater but for honest perspective. In our case, counsel engagement (October 2023) and the legal separation process (completed November 1, 2023) were crucial structural steps that allowed the stewardship work to continue without becoming entangled in personal drama. Accountability bodies are not ceremonial; they are lifeboats when the water gets rough.

- Don't romanticize sacrifice. Sacrifice has to be strategic. Sacrificial stories make good speeches. Sustained sacrifice without strategy makes good obituaries. Sacrifice that's planned, measured, and shared is sustainable. Sacrifice that's romanticized and solitary is not.

Pocket Rules and Practical Moves

- Steward your capacity, you can only protect what you can still hold.

- Defend people publicly; correct privately. Preserve dignity; reduce collateral damage.

- Say your limits out loud. When others know what you'll carry, they can carry the rest.

- Raise and protect deputies. Elevate people who can stand in the gap; shield them when they do.

- Make repair real, not performative. Own the miss; fix the process; move forward.

- Triage your fights. Conserve steward energy for battles that matter.

- Lean on counsel and board accountability when the conflict is structural. Use them to keep personal politics from becoming the operator of your decision-making.

Final word, The Long View

The shield without the mirror becomes an obituary. The mirror without the shield becomes paralysis. The work is ordinary and costly, made of thousands of small decisions that add up to safety or collapse.

If you intend to be a steward, learn two things well: how to stand in the gap so people have a place to do their work, and how to read your own capacity honestly so you can do that work tomorrow as well as today. Protect people, but protect yourself enough so the protection can last.

This chapter grew out of mistakes I made and then fixed. Take these moves as repairs that actually worked, not theory, not slogans. Learn from the failure I lived through so you don't have to learn by the same bruises.

Chapter 22
Operationalizing Voice

Theology

Voice is how standards become visible. If you cannot hear what's true on the floor, your standards are only aspirations on paper; if you can, standards become the air everyone breathes. Operationalizing voice is not a nice-to-have program. It is a Fundamental: a moral claim about who belongs, a stewardship responsibility, and the habit that determines whether standards actually guide daily work. The pattern is simple and unforgiving: invite people in, protect them when they speak, and close the loop visibly. Do those three things and feedback becomes fuel; skip them and you harvest silence.

Gallup looked at more than 140,000 employees and found what most leaders already know by instinct: when people have a safe, predictable way to speak up, the whole room gets stronger. Productivity rises. Great people stay. Trust becomes normal instead of rare. The absence of voice produces the opposite: rising burnout and voluntary exits.

Silence isn't neutral; it's expensive. Every unspoken concern adds unseen cost until truth becomes unaffordable. Building systems for voice isn't about compliance, it's about keeping standards alive in the places leadership can't see.

Pocket rule: Silence compounds faster than mistakes.

Why This Matters

Standards tell people what we expect. Voice tells us whether those standards are true. Stewardship demands that when someone tells you the standard is broken or suggests a better standard, you do something about it. Presence means leaders make it safe to speak and then prove the organization can respond. There are two kinds of voice you must court: promotive voice (ideas that move you forward) and prohibitive voice (concerns that prevent harm). Both need psychological safety to sprout. But safety alone is worthless unless you can convert what you hear into repair or change. That conversion, Invite → Protect → Close, is the Fundamental. Tools exist only to make that conversion ordinary and durable.

Google's long-term Project Aristotle research and a 2023 Harvard Business Review follow-up confirmed that psychological safety is the strongest predictor of both innovation and retention. Teams that felt safe to raise concerns or propose change were 50 percent more likely to launch new ideas and 31 percent less likely to experience turnover. The common factor was not optimism but follow-through: employees trusted what they could see leaders act on.

Safety is the soil; response is the harvest. Without visible action, even the bravest voices stop speaking.

Pocket rule: Safety invites truth; response keeps it alive.

Stories

A New Department & A Bad Idea

We learned this the practical way: by watching voice, either build us up or expose a blind spot.

When the team proposed a Project Management function, I backed it. I hired Kahlie to lead the work, and we built the processes together. Giving the work named owners and predictable rhythms stopped the slow bleed of missed handoffs. The immediate result was fewer dropped balls and less rework; the longer result was steadier capacity and lower burnout. That change came from the floor; leadership's visible backing turned an idea into a durable practice. That is, voice becoming a capability.

Deloitte's 2023 Human Capital Trends report found that organizations that convert employee suggestions into funded, measurable initiatives deliver 33 percent faster implementation and sustain 26 percent lower burnout across twelve months. The differentiator was structure: when leadership linked promotive voice to resources, employees stopped seeing feedback as "extra" and started treating it as part of the job.

Voice is not noise to manage; it's capacity waiting for an outlet. When truth rises from the floor and leadership backs it with resources, the organization compounds energy instead of losing it to repetition.

Pocket rule: Fund the voices you claim to value.

A different kind of lesson came when a staff member pointed out that an apartment we were considering as an office included bedrooms. This made her uncomfortable, and rightly so. We hadn't fully considered how that setup could be interpreted or what boundaries it might unintentionally complicate. We did an immediate about-face, no pause, no delay, and changed course. That swift correction preserved trust, but the near-miss exposed a gap: we had no simple standard for how workplace spaces should serve everyone. The fix was procedural and simple, but the lesson was moral, if you do not build rules that protect people, good intentions will still fail the people they claim to serve. And the immediate about-face prevented the deeper erosion of trust that happens when concerns are minimized or delayed.

MIT Sloan tracked thousands of employees who raised ethical concerns and found something simple and sobering: when leaders act fast, trust grows. When leaders delay, minimize, or explain the concern away, trust erodes, sometimes by half, and it happens even when no actual harm occurred. The speed of the response is what tells people whether their voice matters.

Moral stewardship is proven in speed and simplicity. Correction doesn't need a speech; it needs visible alignment between values and action. That is how standards move from policy to culture.

Pocket rule: Swift repair is the loudest statement of values.

These two examples are not showpieces. They are proof. One shows how promotive voice becomes capacity when leaders act and resource; the other shows how prohibitive voice prevents harm when the organization treats it as urgent, not optional. The difference between the two cases was not whether the voices were right, it was how we treated them.

Takeaways

Pattern & Principles, Invite → Protect → Close

- Invite. Make speaking up ordinary. Don't make it a favor or an audition. An invitation is a posture: routine, low-friction, and public enough that it becomes ordinary.

- Protect. Shield the speaker. Publicly back them when they are right and handle corrective work privately so dignity is preserved. Protection is stewardship in the small things: it is choosing the uncomfortable moment now so the team can survive the long haul.

- Close. Close the loop. If a person brings you a problem and you don't visibly act, or at least clearly explain why no action is possible, you erode trust. Closing is not theater. It is the discipline of follow-through: name the owner, set the due date, and report back.

Pocket line: Invite with humility. Protect with courage. Close with clarity.

What this Fundamental looks like in practice

This is not a menu to pick from. It is a single pattern expressed in a handful of repeatable moves. If you want the full, copy-ready templates, that belongs in the playbook. Here, the chapter keeps it to what matters and what proves the point.

Make the invitation ordinary. Create small, recurring ways for people to speak that do not feel like risk, a short skip-level cadence, a whiteboard where problems are triaged weekly, or a monthly "what worked / what didn't" that gives promotive and prohibitive voice equal weight. The point is predictability: when speaking up is routine, it stops being dramatic.

Protect the person who speaks. Publicly restate the standard and take the heat; correct privately. If someone raises a safety concern, treat it like a safety issue, raise it quickly, keep the reporter informed, and remove exposure. If someone proposes an experiment, test it with guards, not with blame. The public-protect / private-correct posture is small and simple, but it sustains dignity.

Close visibly and credibly. Every intake must have an owner and a visible next step. If you can't act, explain why. If you can act, do it, and then report the result. Closure is the deposit in the trust ledger; it is how trust gets counted.

Make governance plain. Decide who sees escalation cases, and what triggers counsel or board oversight. Safety and structural risk must bypass local politics. Clear triggers and a facts-only escalation format keep the work from becoming personal theater.

Teach leaders how to receive. Coaching is not just for the frontline; leaders need rehearsal. Practice three moves: listen without defending, restate to confirm, commit to next steps and deadlines. Rehearse that language until it does not feel awkward.

The Ritual That Proves The Pattern

We needed a single ritual that connected invitation to closure without creating a new bureaucracy. What we landed on was small and stubborn: a monthly thirty-minute leaders' session with a strict agenda and real commitments. The session begins with ten minutes of quick wins and recognition so the meeting does not become only a complaint forum. The middle ten minutes are raw: named issues, one sentence apiece, no backstory. The final ten minutes are mechanics: who owns what, and what the next concrete step looks like.

I committed, personally, to two simple promises for anything that came through that room. First, a written acknowledgment within seventy-two hours so people knew they were heard. Second, an ownership assignment within fourteen days so items did not live forever as "maybe." The Project Management team used the session's outputs to drive the work that otherwise got lost. Kahlie's team would take a named issue off the whiteboard, triage it into the case flow, and show the first fix in two weeks. Suddenly, the room stopped tolerating "we'll get to it" and started counting deposits of trust.

That ritual also lets us practice protection. When someone in the session described a gripe that had been aired publicly, I learned to restate the standard out loud, a one-line public defense, and then move the correction offline. Guardianship like that is not theatrical: it is custody. It says, in front of the people, that we will not let the loudest voices destroy the dignity of the quiet ones.

The reason the ritual matters is simple. It routinizes invitation. It forces follow-through. It makes protecting the leader's job in the moment. And because it was small, it actually happened. You don't need a committee to do this, you need a chosen cadence, a named owner, and a promise that gets kept.

Common Failure Modes

We learned the worst lessons by watching what silence does. For a while, we ran listening sessions and town halls and then went back to our day jobs. People came, they spoke, and nothing visibly changed. Over time, the room got quieter. That quiet wasn't peace; it was the absence of hope. The fix was not another meeting; it was the ritual above, a predictable, auditable loop that made speaking mean something.

Fear of retaliation is not a theoretical problem. We saw how even well-intended ideas could make people hold back until they felt safe enough to name the cost. The apartment episode might have been significant if we had ignored it; instead, the immediate about-face prevented the deeper erosion of trust that happens when concerns are minimized or delayed. That moment taught us that anti-retaliation is not a policy on paper; it is what you prove with action the minute someone says, "This makes me uncomfortable."

No owner is the lethal omission. Before we had PMs, projects routinely had no single person responsible for completion; tasks leaked between teams and accountability diffused into failure. Naming ownership and expecting a first visible step within a short time window is the single operational habit that turned work from rumor into result.

Multiple channels without triage create noise that buries the signal. Early on, we had reports coming to different inboxes and no single place to see what remained open. That meant people re-reported the same friction and leaders thought the problem was less urgent because it appeared in many forms. Bringing intake to one board and tagging each item with a type and owner made it auditable; that change came from PM discipline and the culture of keeping commitments.

Finally, anonymity must be handled carefully. It is essential for safety, and we used anonymous intake where needed. But relying on anonymity because leadership could not or would not act hides the real problem, leadership's unwillingness to bear short-term heat in order to keep trust long-term. So our rule became simple: default to named voice for speed and repair; provide anonymity when safety demands it; and when anonymity is used, escalate to confidential intake and counsel review immediately so someone is accountable for action.

The cost of failing at any of these things is not a spreadsheet line. It is quiet people walking away, small harms that become norms, and the slow corrosion of the culture you thought you were protecting.

Strategic Closure, Measurement, Governance, and Stewardship

We learned that operationalizing voice without measurement is faith, not practice. Early on, it felt odd to announce metrics for something as tender as trust, but the ledger is practical: visible behavior needs visible accountability. We started tracking a couple of simple indicators, response time and visible ownership, because they answered the only useful question: are we closing the loop? The PM team held us to those numbers in the way a good coach holds an athlete to form; the board asked for redacted, regular updates so they could see system-level risk instead of headline drama. That oversight did not replace judgment; it made judgment cleaner. It put a boundary between daily heat and structural review.

Gallup found the same pattern we kept seeing on the ground: when leaders actually track trust, response times, ownership, follow-through, accountability rises and teams work together instead of around each other. The numbers were striking, but the point was simple: what you measure, you protect. What you leave to chance eventually leaks.

Metrics don't cheapen trust; they protect it from amnesia. When leaders publish response and closure rates, voice stays credible because results stay visible.

Pocket rule: Track trust like a budget and it stops leaking.

This is also where the Shield & Mirror work matters. Operationalizing voice will demand labor, and leaders must watch the ledger of their own capacity. If the leader is the only shield, the system is brittle. Part of the measurement work is counting the human cost and ensuring deputies exist and are protected, not exposed. That is stewardship: build systems that let voice survive your absence and your limits.

Pocket rules

- Invite. Protect. Close, repeat it until it sounds like a habit.

- Make ownership visible: name the owner and the next step within 14 days.

- Publicly defend; correct privately. That single posture preserves dignity.

- Rehearse leaders to receive; practice beats good intention.

Final line

The Project Management Team taught us how voice could become capacity; the apartment near-miss taught us what happens when process lags compassion. Operationalizing voice is ordinary, not heroic: small, disciplined moves that make speaking safe and make answers visible. Do those small things and you stop managing drama and start stewarding a culture that actually hears.

Chapter 23

Sustainable Servant

Servant leadership isn't martyrdom. It's stewardship.

If I burn the engine to rescue everyone else, the mission loses me, and everything I was supposed to carry. That isn't noble; it's negligent. A servant who runs on empty becomes another problem to solve. A leader who confuses sacrifice with self-destruction eventually teaches the wrong lesson: collapse is the price of caring.

Sustainability isn't softness. It's what keeps standards alive and presence steady. If leadership is stewardship, then capacity, sleep, recovery, spiritual life, family, and health are part of what I steward. Capacity is an asset. Treat it that way.

Everything we now know about burnout confirms what experience already taught me: exhaustion isn't a badge of honor. Modern workforce studies show the same pattern, burnout rises when demand outpaces recovery and falls when leaders design margin on purpose. Capacity isn't indulgence; it's infrastructure. You can't scale depletion and call it excellence.

Steward capacity, like capital, compounds or collapses.

Burnout isn't weakness; it's a design flaw. It happens when the system around a leader rewards endless demand but never protects recovery. It's not cured by slogans about balance. It's prevented by building recovery practices that treat energy as a managed resource.

If burnout is recurring, fix design, not people.

Design matters. Pressure is unavoidable, but pressure without recovery breaks people. When leaders treat rest like a resource and margin like maintenance, the standard holds. When they don't, the standard erodes.

Biology has limits. Neuroscience and performance research have shown for years that sleep loss dulls judgment the same way alcohol does. If you wouldn't lead a room buzzed, don't lead it sleep-deprived. Clarity is moral, not cosmetic.

Exhaustion distorts judgment; rest restores truth.

Servant leadership has always valued awareness and stewardship, both impossible if you erase yourself in the process. Boundaries aren't barriers; they're fences that protect fruit. A servant without them eventually feeds others from an empty field.

Boundaries are how humility stays healthy.

I didn't grasp all this in 2022 or 2023. I learned it slowly, across 2024 and into 2025, through counseling, honest mirrors, and finally admitting I'd run on red for too long. What follows is what I practice now and what I teach, not a rewrite of history.

If there was heat, I closed the distance. Not as a tactic, by instinct.

I like to climb mountains. Not the harness-and-rope kind that leaves you hanging over the abyss, but the steady kind, boots, backpack, trail, air that thins with every step. I've been doing it since the late 1990s. In July 2011, I was on Mt. Whitney in California, the highest peak in the lower forty-eight.

We were maybe half a mile up the trail when someone ahead yelled, "Bear!" Then I heard it too, crashing through the trees, heavy and fast, coming down the hill. The sound was primal. It passed within fifty feet of us, just a blur of muscle and motion. Instinct took over. I threw my pack down, grabbed my camera, and ran straight down the slope after it, off the trail, toward the river it was probably heading for.

About fifty yards in, reality caught up. *You idiot, you're chasing a bear.* I stopped, tried to steady the shot, and all I caught in the dim morning light was a fuzzy black blob framed by gray streaks of trees. It wasn't courage. It was reflex. Trouble appeared, and I moved toward it. That's how I've always been wired, close distance first, think later.

Back home, a client once tried to throw his size around. He had me by roughly a hundred pounds and a foot and a half. I stood toe-to-toe and made it plain: threats wouldn't move us; I would protect my people. Direct. Calm. Unflinching.

Another day we were in a meeting near the front of our building when bursts outside sounded like automatic gunfire. Everyone moved to the back. I went out the front. It turned out to be a vehicle with a loudspeaker. My first move wasn't analysis; it was standing in the gap.

These aren't trophies. They're proof of a reflex: when trouble appeared, I put myself in front of it. I don't regret protecting people. I regret believing protection always required me, that safety had to wear my face. That design made the culture safe only when I was present. Fragile.

Separate from the no-flight reflex, I built an operating system around stress. The hotter it got, the more I moved. Pressure felt like oxygen, until it didn't.

Without meaning to, I made stress normal. Crisis pays in the short term. It wins applause and lets you skip the slower work of standards and training. But it's expensive. The more fires you put out, the more every spark comes your way. After a while, you aren't just responding to stress, you're sustained by it. The hit of urgency feels like progress even when it's erosion.

Physiologists call it an adrenaline loop; psychologists call it learned urgency. Either way, the science lines up with what I lived: when adrenaline becomes your fuel, calm feels like loss. Recovery isn't indulgence; it's a reset of truth.

Urgency feels like impact until it becomes injury.

There was fear under it, fear of letting people down, of missing something important, of the culture cracking if I slowed down. So I carried more than was mine to carry and called it service.

The bill showed up quietly. My mind stayed clear, but the conversion from clarity to action began to stall. Sleep fractured. Energy came in waves. I could carry a room, then sit alone and feel the drop hit like a curtain.

Counseling helped me name it. My counselor said talking to me felt like talking to a firefighter. She wasn't wrong. I had built a life on showing up in crisis and never built one that let me recover from it.

Therapists and performance coaches describe what I finally learned firsthand: short, structured recovery rituals, breathing, journaling, reflection, and retrain the nervous system. Recovery doesn't soften resolve; it sharpens it. Even a firefighter needs a base to return to. Servant leadership requires the same discipline, build the recovery routine before the next alarm rings.

Reflex needs rest to stay righteous.

From the outside, nothing changed. I still carried rooms. I still shielded people. But refusing to leak became its own leak. When a leader always arrives and never rests, the organization learns two bad lessons: the leader is a bottomless well, and rest is for other people. Both are lies. Both break trust over time.

Leadership research keeps proving the point: when senior leaders model visible rest and hand off recovery time, their teams perform better and trust more. Culture copies what it sees, not what it hears. If leaders never pause, neither will their people, and exhaustion becomes the brand.

Demonstrate rest or you'll duplicate collapse.

Two patterns, one cost. The no-flight reflex put me in harm's way. The stress engine kept me there too long. Together they looked like loyalty. In practice, they were unsustainable. A servant who disappears can't serve. A leader out of gas can't hold standards. And a culture built on one person's surge is already in danger.

Counseling gave me language; reflection gave me options. I saw the pattern clearly and accepted that change wasn't optional. I began building balance I could actually keep: less chasing, more design; more sleep and quiet, fewer adrenaline commitments; handing lanes to operators and protecting a little margin.

Designing margin isn't laziness, it's maintenance of mission. Systems that breathe keep standards alive; systems packed to capacity suffocate them.

Prune for purpose before pressure prunes you.

Bob Goff's "Quit Something Thursday" gave me permission to create capacity on purpose so the work that matters can breathe.

The other piece was learning to carry pain without drowning in it. Empathy without boundaries turns to absorption; compassion carries care without carrying the shock. I started practicing small resets between heavy conversations, breathing, brief prayer, short pauses, so the moment would leave my body. It didn't make me less present; it kept me available for tomorrow.

Presence that persists requires margin between moments. It is not detachment; it is design.

Compassion sustains; absorption erodes.

None of this softened the mission. It stabilized it. The mission deserves durability, not drama. My family deserves a husband and father who isn't a ghost on the couch. The future of work requires leaders who can show up next year with a clean mind and a clean standard.

Treat capacity like a ledger. Inputs, sleep, movement, nutrition, prayer, quiet, family, either deposit or they don't. Outputs, conflict triage, hard decisions, public pressure, withdraw. When withdrawals outrun deposits long enough, you lose judgment and presence. Track it. If the line is red, fix inputs before adding outputs.

Design so that demand meets resources. List the demands you can't avoid and the resources you can raise: quiet blocks, operator triage, recovery days, counseling, and honest mirrors. The goal isn't zero demand; it's balance. Schedule resources like a budget line.

Build a conflict intake; stop chasing fires. Publish a one-page lane: route, triage, assign, follow-up. Step in briefly, then strengthen the system that should handle it next time. Your job isn't to be the only shield; it's to create shields.

Engineer space on purpose. Make margin a system, not a mood. I use a short capacity check each week: Does this advance our standard? Would I say yes again today? Should an operator own this instead of me? If not, I quit it, delegate it, or time-box it.

Practice compassion, not contagion. Be fully present without carrying everyone's panic in your body. Short resets between heavy moments build durability.

Use accountability as a mirror, not a stage. Three monthly questions: Am I sleeping? What did I say no to? What standard did we formalize that removed a recurring fire? I keep people close who will ask me these questions and tell me the truth even when it's hard. Accountability isn't exposure; it's maintenance. A mirror held in love lets leaders keep showing up whole.

Accountability is how humility stays in shape.

Make rhythms non-negotiable. Protect real sleep, movement, and family time. Treat violations as process failures, not badges of honor. Heroics spark admiration; rhythms sustain mission. The leader who guards a healthy pattern guards the future of everyone they serve.

Keep the rhythm and the rhythm will keep you.

Free the operators. Write the standard. Train for it. Inspect it. Then let operators carry the room. If every escalation still requires you, you don't have a team, you have an audience. Delegation isn't surrender; it's proof of trust. When operators are freed to lead, stewardship scales beyond one person's endurance.

Delegation is the loudest form of trust.

Document your shield moments. After every time you step in, write a short after-action: why you stepped in, what it cost, and what will change upstream. Reflection turns reaction into improvement.

If you don't write the lesson, the wound will reteach it.

Choose signal over spotlight when it's hot. Don't feed conflict with attention. State the standard. Enforce it. Move on. Standards change cultures; names distort them. Keep names out of it. Keep the wrong motives vapor.

Shine light on standards, not on yourself.

This Fundamental isn't about proving I'm fearless. It's about staying available to my family, my team, and the future of the work. I used to think loyalty meant never slowing down and always standing in the doorway. I know better now. Loyalty means lasting.

I'm still the guy who moves toward trouble when I need to. I just don't pretend I'm the only one who can, and I don't pretend I can do it forever. My promise now is simple: protect the standard, guard the people, and steward the capacity to show up again tomorrow.

Less surge, more system. Less me, more we.

That's the shape of a sustainable servant.

Lasting is how we lead.

Chapter 24

Landing the Plane

I didn't write this to prove I made it through. I wrote it so the next leader in the room has something they can do.

The thesis of this book is simple: leadership is stewardship.

Own the standard. Be present. Enforce quietly. Make it possible for other people to do good work. That spine runs under every shard in Part 1 and every Fundamental in Part 2.

Part 1 showed what happens when standards drift and rooms rely on personalities. It showed what presence costs and why restraint matters, keeping names vapor, refusing spectacle, letting the work speak.

Part 2 gave language and handles: Do the Work. Protect the Culture. Clarity Beats Chaos. Empowerment Over Control. Sacrifice Builds Influence. Invest in People. Trust as a Daily Currency. Feedback, what to say and how to build the system that lets truth move in every direction. The Shield & the Mirror. Operationalizing Voice. Sustainable Servant so we last.

If you remember nothing else, remember this: standards change cultures; names reveal them. Your job is to write the standard in plain words, live it where others can see it, and enforce it without turning the room into a stage. The rest is logistics.

What this book means for you.

You don't need a bigger brand, a louder voice, or a drama arc. You need a clean standard, a steady presence, and the courage to keep both when keeping them has a cost.

Your team doesn't need a performer. They need an owner who stewards, someone who makes work safer by making rules real.

Noise isn't a strategy. Adrenaline isn't fuel. Systems, tied to standards, carry the room.

The pattern beneath every chapter.

Beneath every scene in Part 1 and every Fundamental in Part 2 is the same loop. It isn't flashy. It's how cultures actually change.

1. Show up and do the work (receipts over rhetoric).

2. Presence first. Proof beats promises. If you can't point to how the standard lives today, you don't have a standard; you have a copy.

3. State a clean standard and make it visible.

4. Small enough to remember, strong enough to enforce. Write it in the working language. If operators can't say it back, it isn't clear.

5. Protect people by protecting the rules (quiet enforcement).

6. Standards change cultures; names reveal them. Praise in public, correct in private, keep villains vapor. No theater. Just the rule and the next right step.

7. Design lanes so heat runs on process, not adrenaline.

8. Route → triage → assign → follow-up. Name owners. Close loops. When you must step in, step out quickly and leave a stronger lane behind.

9. Tell the truth fast and in every direction.

10. Feedback isn't a moment; it's a system. Up, down, across. Say the hard things well and build the channels that move truth

without drama.

11. Build trust like a ledger, small deposits, every day.

12. Keep the promises you make, especially the small ones. Inspect your own ledger first. Influence arrives on the receipts of reliability.

13. Grow people and give them the room (empowerment over control).

14. Train, inspect, and hand off real decisions. If every escalation still requires you, you don't have a team, you have an audience.

15. Practice the Shield & the Mirror.

16. Protect your people in public. Hold the mirror to yourself in private. Take the hit they can't take; own the miss you did make.

17. Operationalize voice so the culture can speak without you.

18. Codify how you decide, how you coach, how you close loops. Not scripts, patterns. When the voice is portable, the culture travels.

19. Guard capacity so you can repeat tomorrow (sustainable servant).

20. Rhythm beats heroics. Sleep, movement, prayer, family, quiet. Capacity is an asset, steward it. You can't be the shield if you're broken.

That's the engine under everything you've read: standard → presence → enforcement → systems → truth → trust → empowerment → accountability → voice → endurance. Run that loop and the room stops depending on your personality and starts depending on the work.

How to move your room, starting now.

You don't need an overhaul by Friday. You need to move the room one standard at a time.

Start with words you'll keep.

Choose the few behaviors that define your place. Write them where people can see them, in working language. Ask operators to say them back in their own words. If it sounds like a poster, you wrote it wrong. If it sounds like work, you wrote it right.

Install lanes so problems stop defaulting to you.

Publish your heat intake: route $\rightarrow$ triage $\rightarrow$ assign $\rightarrow$ follow-up. Name owners. Make "how we handle trouble" a rule, not a rumor. The first time a fire clears the lane without you, say so out loud. That's how trust in the system starts.

Make feedback part of the air.

Use one stem: "Here's the standard. Here's what I saw. Here's what happens next." Invite the same back to you. Up, down, across. Truth moves fast in healthy rooms; that's why they don't boil.

Free the operators.

Pick two decisions you still make by reflex that an operator should own. Teach. Shadow. Hand off. Inspect. If it boomerangs, your handoff was a speech, not a transfer.

Protect the capacity that makes all of this possible.

Put recovery on the calendar like revenue. Say a clean no to something that doesn't serve the standard. Tell your team why you said no. You're not modeling comfort; you're modeling endurance.

None of this needs a stage. It needs consistency, doing the same unglamorous things until the room expects them and protects them without you.

If You're Leading on Fumes.

I did it for too long. If that's you:

- Name what's true. Stress isn't oxygen. Call it what it is.

- Make one boundary visible. Keep it for two weeks.

- Quit one obligation that doesn't serve the standard. Clean no.

- Give one shield away. Teach an operator the thing you still stand in front of. Stay close; don't stay central.

- Tell your team what you're changing and why. They don't need heroics; they need you to last.

This isn't stepping back from responsibility. It's stepping toward it with a steadier hand.

What I'd Have You Carry

Signal over spotlight.

If it doesn't serve the mission, it doesn't get the mic.

Standards over personalities.

Write them, teach them, enforce them, then let the work become the authority instead of the leader.

Not everyone in the room will choose the standard,

but the standard must still stand.

Don't amplify the dysfunction, reinforce the rule.

When the rule is clear, the noise eventually has nowhere to root itself.

You don't protect culture by wrestling with every disruption.

You protect culture by anchoring it so deeply that disruption can only skim the surface.

Correct privately. Uphold publicly.

Let the standard, not the storyteller, shape the room.

Presence over performance.

Show up steady. Show up clearly. Show up again tomorrow.

Rhythm beats heroics every time.

Guard the capacity that keeps you whole.

Sleep, move, pray, think. Protect the well so it never runs dry.

Capacity isn't comfort, it's stewardship.

These aren't slogans.

They're rails.

They keep you from drifting when the weather turns.

The Close

If you're still here, then you already understand the truth:

cultures aren't built by larger-than-life founders.

They're built by leaders who stay steady long enough to make the work real.

So here's the charge, simple, demanding, and entirely within your reach:

- Write a standard your team can trust.

- Build lanes that let the work run without you.

- Tell the truth quickly and kindly.

- Guard your capacity so tomorrow has a leader.

Do those things on repeat and you'll create a room where people can breathe, work, and grow, not because of your personality, not because of your intensity, but because the structure you steward makes it safe to do good work.

That is the quiet power of stewardship.

It removes the spotlight, strengthens the spine,

and makes it possible for the mission to outlive the moment.

This is the work.

This is the way we lead.

This is how we last.